MONSTERS
UNLEASHED

Bugging
Out

MON UNL

Bugging Out

JOHN KLOEPFER

ILLUSTRATED BY
MARK OLIVER

HARPER
An Imprint of HarperCollins*Publishers*

Library of Congress Control Number: 2017949547
ISBN 978-0-06-242753-3 (trade bdg.)

Typography by Aurora Parlagreco
18 19 20 21 22 LSCH/CG 10 9 8 7 6 5 4 3 2 1

First Edition

To Gemma, my very own furry, four-legged monster

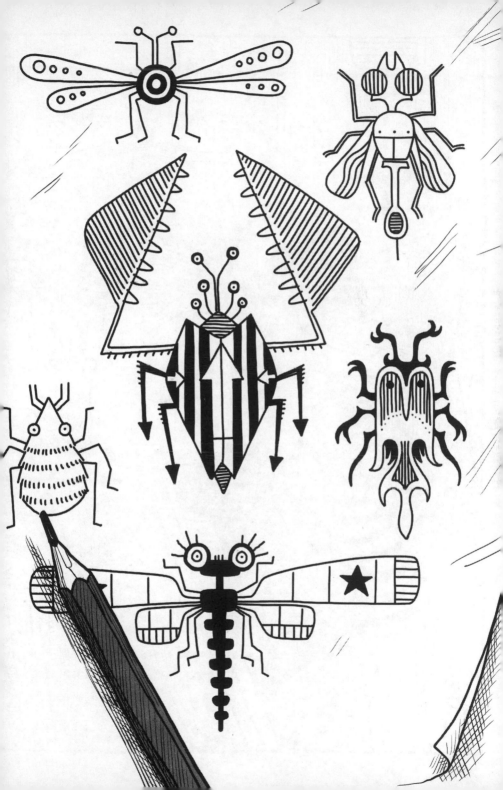

1

Freddie Liddle was back in art class. His seat was too small for him, and his back hurt from being hunched over his latest drawing. It was like nothing had changed—except everything was different. He and his friends were at a new school with new kids and new teachers.

There was a good reason for this.

Two weeks ago Freddie and his best friend and fellow outcast, Manny Vasquez, had accidentally created a trio of monsters using their then art teacher's 3D printer. The monsters were based on Freddie's drawings of the three meanest bullies in his class: Jordan Cross, the jock; Nina Green, the drama queen; and, last but never least, Quincy Moorehead, the know-it-all.

1

These humongous monsters had destroyed their middle school, and nearly their entire town, before the kids managed to shrink them down.

Freddie knew it sounded unbelievable.

But even harder to swallow was that Freddie and his former bullies were all cool with one another now. For the first time in his life, Freddie had a real group of friends. And they also had pet minimonsters, which at the moment were stashed in Freddie's closet. Before they could go home to their monsters, though, they had to get through the rest of the school day.

At least they were in art class, Freddie's favorite subject. In the back of the room, Freddie was sitting next to Manny. He watched as Manny's light-brown hand doodled on a piece of paper. They were working on a page of their ongoing comic book that they were always tinkering with, but Manny seemed distracted.

Finally, Manny put his pencil down and gestured to a kid at the end of the art table. The kid was scribbling angrily on his sketch pad. It looked like he was drawing some kind of weird insect, erasing it, then starting

over until his paper was nothing more than a bunch of smudges and pink crumbs from his eraser. The more he tried to draw, the more frustrated he became.

"This guy is having some serious artist's block," Manny said. "It's freaking me out. I can't concentrate."

Freddie felt bad for the kid, so he went over and tapped him on the shoulder. "Hey, man, chill out," he said. "Don't draw angry."

The kid looked up at Freddie. He was clearly flustered.

"Ugh. I hate art," the boy groaned. "I can see what I

want to draw, but I can't draw it." He paused. "My name is Trevor, by the way. Trevor Kelso."

Freddie put out his hand. "Freddie Liddle," he said. "And this is Manny."

Manny didn't even look up. His long black hair fell over his eyes. "Yo."

"Wow, you're pretty good!" Trevor said, glancing over at Freddie's open sketchbook. He paused for a second. "Hey, do you think you could draw this idea for me?" Trevor asked Freddie. "I'd pay you for it. . . ."

"He doesn't draw anything for less than forty bucks," Manny said.

"That's pretty steep," Trevor said. "All I've got is twenty dollars."

Trevor pulled out the bill from his pocket. His fingers were long and knobby. In fact, the rest of Trevor was gawky and gangly, too, all knees and elbows. He had big hair that swooped behind each ear and fell just a couple inches short of his shoulders. He had a small forehead and long thin eyebrows, big bug eyes, pale white skin, and a long pointy nose. Freddie felt bad for the kid. At twelve years old and over six feet tall,

Freddie had been made fun of a lot. He knew what it was like to be an outsider.

"That's okay," Freddie said. "No charge."

"You should consider yourself very lucky," Manny said to Trevor. "Freddie's drawing could be very valuable one day."

Freddie couldn't tell if his pal was being sarcastic or not. The last week or so, since they'd become friends with their former bullies, Manny had been acting strangely. And today he didn't seem like himself at all.

Trevor murmured something under his breath neither of them could hear, then crumpled up his botched drawing and tossed it on the floor. He started to write up a page of instructions with all the traits and features he wanted his weird made-up insect creature to have: camouflage armor, razor spikes, lightning-fast grappling claws, venomous fangs, chomping mandible. The list went on and on.

"Its name will be entomon," Trevor announced to them. "That's Greek for *insect*."

"No waaaay . . . ," Manny said in a long-drawn-out monotone.

Freddie definitely sensed the sarcasm in his voice this time.

Freddie studied the sheet that Trevor had given him and started to sketch the outline of the hybrid insect.

"Yes, that's it exactly!" Trevor exclaimed as Freddie drew the basic shape. "I wish I could draw like you."

Trevor watched over Freddie's shoulder as he drew. Freddie did his best to make the entomon look as cool and as scary as possible. He drew its body like a cross between a beetle and an ant. The sleek blue-black bug had a hard shiny shell, pincers and claws and giant mandibles almost twice the size of its head. If Freddie had seen it on the wall of his bedroom, he probably would've peed in his pants.

"This is so cool," Trevor said. "Thanks!"

"Sure, buddy," Freddie told him, glad to be helping the kid out.

The bell rang and Trevor snatched the drawing off the table with a gleam in his eyes. "Pleasure doing business with you, big guy," he said with a wink as he hustled out of the art room.

Freddie and Manny watched him go. "I wonder why he's in such a rush," Freddie said.

"He must be late for loser club," Manny replied as he packed up his stuff. He glanced at the clock. "Oh shoot! I have to get to gym or else Mr. Felzer's gonna make me run laps," He rushed out into the hallway.

Across the art room, Jordan, Nina, and Quincy gathered their things and walked over to Freddie.

"What was that all about?" asked Quincy.

"That kid's a little strange. He's in my science class, too," Nina said, nodding at where Trevor had just been sitting. She pushed back her thick braids and scrunched her nose. "He's obsessed with bugs. His binder has pictures of centipedes all over it."

"I know!" Jordan said. He had a smudge of paint on his brown cheek. "I saw that he has one with spiders all over it, too."

"C'mon, guys, give him a break," Freddie said. "You

don't know what it's like to be a loner."

"True. That's why we keep you around, Freddie," Quincy said. "So, are we all good to go to your house after school and check up on our minimonsters? Mega-Q gets cranky if he doesn't get a snack by four o'clock."

"Yeah, my dad should be out of the house by then," Freddie said. "He's working a double shift tonight at the factory."

Jordan, Nina, and Quincy nodded in approval.

"Let's meet up by the vending machines after the last bell," Jordan said.

Freddie was getting used to his new after-school routine. It wasn't just him and Manny goofing off anymore. He had new friends, a new school, and new monsters to take care of. Life would be perfect if it stayed just as it was right now.

He'd never felt so happy and relaxed in his life.

The last bell of the day finally blared through the school, and a mob of students poured out of the classrooms.

Freddie met up with Nina at the water fountain. He looked down at her. Her dark brown skin was flawless, her braids were cool, and she was wearing an awesome outfit. He couldn't believe he was hanging out with the most popular girl in his class. It was like Freddie was suddenly royalty.

He looked over the top of the crowd and quickly spotted Jordan and Quincy by the vending machines. Nina and Freddie worked their way through the heavy foot traffic clogging up the locker-lined hallway. By the time they got to the vending machines, Jordan had already gobbled down half a bag of beef jerky.

"Can I have a piece?" Quincy asked, putting out his pale, freckled hand.

"I don't see why I should give you anything," Jordan said with a mouthful of jerky, "when you didn't give me the answers to our math homework."

"That's called cheating," Nina said as she and Freddie sidled up to the two boys. "Where's that going to get you in life?"

"Umm . . . on the honor roll?" Jordan said, still chewing with his mouth open.

Out of the crowd, Manny appeared, heading straight for them. He screeched to a halt in front of them, clutching his knees and catching his breath. He had an odd look in his eyes.

"You guys . . . you have to see this." Manny huffed and puffed. "That kid Trevor . . . from art class . . . somehow . . . he's got some kind of monster . . . of his own. . . ."

Manny held up his phone, and they peered at the video on the screen.

He tapped the play icon and the video started.

The movie was shaky at first, like Manny was hiding

behind a door or something. As the camera steadied, they could see Trevor in the locker room. They watched as Trevor dropped his backpack off his shoulders and sat on the bench.

"Gross!" Nina exclaimed. "I don't want to see this dude get changed!"

"Just watch . . . ," Manny said.

Freddie peered at the touch screen, as Trevor pulled something out of his backpack. It was a glass mason jar. And inside the glass were *two* identical bug creatures that looked exactly like what Freddie had drawn for Trevor that morning.

Trevor's eyes were filled with love as he rocked his monsters in his arms like they were his precious little babies.

Freddie's head was swimming with so many questions, he could barely think. Were those just bugs? Or were they really . . . bug monsters? *How did this happen?* There was only one possible answer, and Freddie didn't like it.

"He must have the printer," Freddie muttered under his breath. But his friends were so focused on the bugs they didn't hear him.

"What are those things?" Jordan shuddered.

"Those are entomons," Manny said. "It means *insect* in Greek."

"I know what it means," Quincy said. "But that doesn't look like any bug I've ever seen."

"It's not," Manny said. "That's because Freddie drew them."

"You did *what*?" Nina squeaked.

Freddie pinched the bridge of his wide, white-skinned nose. "In art class today, Trevor asked me to draw him this bug monster. He said he wasn't talented enough to draw it himself," Freddie said. "He must have known about us and the printer and our monsters, because how else would he have made those from my drawing?"

"This is not okay," Quincy said. "As president of monster club, this is UNacceptable."

"First of all, you're not the president," Nina said. "But you're right. This isn't acceptable."

"Come on, let's go find this kid," Jordan said and took off, pushing his way through the crowded hallway.

They raced back toward the boys' locker room. But when they popped their heads inside, the locker room was empty. Trevor and his two bugs were already gone. The kids dashed back out into the hall and almost missed Trevor slipping around the corner.

"Hey, Trevor, wait up!" Nina hollered at him.

The spindly-limbed kid stopped and glanced back. His eyes bugged out when he saw them. Then he took off running.

"Hey!" Manny shouted.

Freddie and the gang hustled after him, but when they rounded the corner, Trevor was nowhere in sight. "Come on—maybe we can catch him out front," said Freddie.

They cut through the center of the building, beelining toward the front entrance. The hall was packed with students hunched over with heavy backpacks.

Sometimes, Freddie thought, *it came in handy being twelve years old and six foot four*. This was one of those times. Peering over everyone's heads, Freddie spotted

Trevor sneaking through the crowd.

"Follow him!" Freddie pointed toward the side exit. He zigzagged through the end-of-the-day mob and accidentally bumped into a group of kids.

"Hey, watch where you're going, freak!" Freddie heard one of them say as he ran outside. Freddie ignored the dig and swiveled his head, looking up and down the street. "There he is!" he shouted.

"Where?" Jordan squinted in the bright sunlight. Manny pointed across the street. "Right over there!"

"Where?" Nina said with her hand over her eyes like a visor.

"I see him!" Quincy yelled. His white skin was flushing in the sun. It almost matched his fiery red hair.

Just as they were about to chase after him, a long yellow school bus vroomed by. The bus passed and Trevor was . . . gone.

"Now where the heck did he go?" asked Freddie.

Manny pointed down the street. Trevor was on a skateboard, hitching a ride on the bus's back bumper.

Freddie's stomach plunged as the bus drove off, taking Trevor with it. The bug-loving kid had no idea how dangerous those creatures could be.

Things were about to get messy again. And unless Freddie and his friends got those monsters back fast, they were going to have to clean things up . . . again.

The five friends walked to Freddie's house to check on their own monsters. Freddie's dad was already gone, so they had the place to themselves.

"I can't believe that little dorkstain is making his own monsters," Nina said, slamming the front door behind them. "With *our* printer."

"I still don't know how he got into your old locker," Jordan said. "The lock wasn't even broken." The kids had made a pit stop at their former middle school on the way to Freddie's. The building was destroyed, but they were able to find Freddie's locker. It was where he had hidden the monster-making 3D printer for safekeeping.

When they checked inside the locker, the printer was gone.

"Maybe if you didn't keep your combination written on the back of the lock, then Trevor wouldn't have been able to get the printer," Manny said.

Freddie glared at his best friend. He hadn't been planning to share that little detail with their other friends.

Jordan, Nina, and Quincy all stopped and stared at Freddie.

"Are you serious?" Quincy said. He grabbed his bright red hair in frustration and pulled, nearly yanking it out. "You can't remember your own locker combo?"

"I always get it mixed up!" Freddie said defensively and then turned to Manny. "Did you have to tell them?"

"Forget about it—what's done is done," Nina said. "Let's go check on the minimonsters and figure out what we're going to do about this Trevor kid."

They went upstairs to Freddie's room and Freddie pulled Manny aside. "Dude, what's your problem?"

"My problem?" Manny asked innocently. "I don't have a problem. Maybe you're the one with the problem."

"You've been acting like this since I hung out with Jordan the other day. Is that what's bothering you?"

"No," Manny said. "Why would I care about that?"

"Because you've been acting strangely ever since then," Freddie said.

Manny fell silent and gave his buddy a shrug.

On the other side of the bedroom, Jordan, Nina, and Quincy opened the closet door, and Nina let out a horrified gasp.

"What is it?" Freddie said, and he and Manny rushed over.

Their five minimonsters were on the floor. Freddie's and Manny's monsters, Oddo and Mungo, were tugging at the last of the gummi worms they had left them. (For some reason, all any of their monsters wanted to eat was gummi candy.) And Jordan's monster, Kraydon, was relaxing; but Nina's and Quincy's monsters, Yapzilla and Mega-Q, were both turned to stone. There were tiny scorch marks all over the carpet. It looked as though some kind of showdown had ended with Kraydon freezing them both.

Jordan's eyebrows furrowed in a V. "Change them back," he ordered Kraydon. The muscle-bound mini-monster stomped his foot, but eventually he swirled his eye and turned them back into living, breathing creatures.

"Sorry about that, guys," Jordan said to Nina and Quincy, as Yapzilla and Mega-Q reanimated.

The five friends brought their monsters to the

kitchen and plopped them on the countertop, while they all helped themselves to the contents of Freddie's snack cupboard and fridge.

"We need a plan," Nina said, biting into an apple. "And I think I know what we have to do."

Nina found the student directory on her iPhone and looked up Trevor's address.

"We gotta get the printer and those monsters back is what we have to do," Jordan said, as he scarfed down a handful of cheese puffs.

"As soon as we get them, we'll have to give them silica," Quincy added, spooning a blob of chocolate pudding into his mouth. For reasons they still couldn't explain, silica pellets had made the monsters shrink down after the exposure to water made them huge.

"Unless they're getting humongous already," Manny said, cracking open a sleeve of Oreos.

The kids all chewed silently for a minute. Freddie imagined the destruction another set of monsters could cause. Half their town was still in shambles. What would happen if they wrecked the other half, too? Freddie couldn't believe Trevor had tricked him into drawing the monsters. And what was worse was Freddie couldn't believe Trevor had figured out how to get his hands on the 3D printer and goo.

He should have been more careful. This was all his fault!

While they ate their after-school snacks, Freddie drew a diagram of the entomon from memory. He showed the new insect monster to Oddo, Mungo, Kraydon, Yapzilla, and Mega-Q. Their minimonsters nodded as Nina explained the plan.

"We'll use your guys' unique abilities to get inside Trevor's house. We'll do it tonight, when everyone's asleep."

"But that would mean that we have to"—Freddie's voice lowered to a whisper—"sneak out of our houses."

"What's your point?" Nina asked him.

"Look at me," Freddie said, towering over the rest of them. "I can't *sneak* anywhere. I'm, like, the worst sneaker in the world! One wrong step and it's Creak City!"

"Wear slippers, then," Nina told him. "We have to go tonight. We can't risk those bugs falling into a toilet or something, and we can't go now because Trevor will be expecting us. We'll meet up after our parents go to sleep."

Lost in his thoughts, Freddie grew more and more worried about their recent string of luck. Or lack of luck. And now that they were sneaking into someone's house, anything could happen. Trevor's parents could catch them and call their parents or even the cops, and then they would all get grounded until they graduated high school. But that was small potatoes compared to their town getting overrun by monster bugs. That, Freddie thought, was a very large potato.

It had been at least an hour since Freddie's dad had come home from work and fallen asleep on the couch. Freddie tiptoed down the steps and heard the wood-saw sound of his father's snoring. He looked down at his feet. Two pink bunny slippers stared up at him. He had followed Nina's advice, except the only slippers he owned were these fluffy pink bunnies. They did seem to work in silencing his footsteps though.

Freddie opened the door without a squeak and slipped outside into the night. Oddo's little monster head poked out of the front pouch pocket of his sweatshirt. Freddie could have sworn his pet monster used to fit

in his pocket more easily. It seemed like he weighed a little more, too. Maybe his sweatshirt had shrunk in the laundry or his monster had eaten too much gummi candy today.

Or both.

Freddie stopped in his tracks as something moved across the sidewalk at his feet. His heart skipped a beat as Mungo chirped up at him. "Yum yums," he said, which was all he ever said. Mungo wore a little black suit and a mask with two eyeholes that made him look like a ninja. Freddie recognized it from one of Manny's action figures. The little monster motioned for Freddie and Oddo to follow him.

As they turned the corner down the street from

his house, Freddie could see all four of his friends waiting in the shadows between the glow of the streetlamps.

"Dude, what are those?" Jordan pointed at Freddie's feet.

"She told me to wear them!" Freddie pointed at Nina.

"Can we get going now, please?" Manny said a little bit testily. "It's after midnight, you know."

They made their way to Trevor's house on Cactus Way. No one spoke for a while as they lurked along the roadside shadows. The whole town was fast asleep.

Quincy broke the silence. "So I did a little research and I think I may have figured out how to feed these things the silica. The entomons appear to be part beetle. Beetles eat slugs, so . . ." Quincy opened up a small tin case filled with slugs. "I took the liberty of making them a snack. I just took a pellet of the silica, which will keep the bug monsters from growing, and pressed the pellet into the slug."

"Nice," Nina said, though Freddie felt his stomach turning. *Nasty.* "My mom does that when our dog has to take a pill. Not with slugs, though."

"Also," Quincy continued, "I watched Manny's video again and figured out what this bug monster is made of. It ain't pretty. I'd hypothesize that they're even stronger than they look. They have these supersharp pincers and, based on the species Trevor combined, I suspect that they're going to be very territorial. He also spliced herbivorous insects with carnivorous insects, so it's probable that they'll eat anything. And since there are two of them, we need to be worried about how they reproduce, which at this point . . . your guess is as good as mine. . . ."

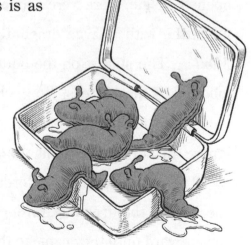

While Jordan and Manny listened to Quincy, Nina sidled up next to Freddie. "Hey," she said. "Are you and Manny okay?"

"Yeah, I think so," Freddie said. "He seems annoyed with me lately, though. Ever since last week."

"Because you have new friends now," she said. "I've been going through the same thing with my friends. They don't understand why I want to spend all my time with you lose—I mean you guys, but I realized after all this stuff with the monsters that my old friends were mean most of the time. You and Manny will be fine. At least he's part of our group, too."

"Thanks, Nina." Freddie smiled.

"Everybody hush up," Jordan said. "We're here!"

They stopped at a red brick two-story house with white shutters and a wooden mailbox, which Freddie opened. Inside, there were a couple of bills and a science magazine with a large dragonfly on the cover, *Insect Monthly*. The sticker on the bottom said Trevor Kelso, followed by the address.

"This is definitely the place," Freddie said, trying to ignore the nervous pit in his stomach.

"The coast is clear . . . ," Jordan whispered and they sneaked up the driveway, through the dark part of the Kelsos' yard until they came to the rear of the house.

They peered at the back door.

Jordan turned to Quincy. "Looks like they have an alarm system. Do you think Mega-Q can take it out?"

Quincy nodded and motioned to Mega-Q, who sent out a pulse of electricity around the house, and they heard a zap as the alarm circuits were disconnected. The tiny green light on the alarm box went off.

"Nice work, buddy," Freddie said to Quincy.

Nice work, buddy, Manny mouthed the words, copying Freddie and making a face.

Jordan turned to Freddie and Manny. "I don't know what's going on with you two, but you better drop it, because this mission is going to take teamwork. We all need to be on the same page of the playbook." He glowered at them both. "Are we all good now?"

"I'm fine," Freddie said sheepishly.

"I'm finer than fine," said Manny. "Never been finer in my life."

Nina cleared her throat. "So how do we get in, then? It's all locked up."

Manny snapped his fingers. "Mungo, go!"

Mungo skulked like a ninja and scaled the brick

siding to the first-floor windowsill. The window locks were all fastened.

Freddie gave Oddo the signal to go help him.

Oddo hopped up after him and wedged his three arms under the locked window frame. He lifted with every ounce of effort in his fluffy round body, and eventually the wood sill bent just enough so Mungo could squeeze underneath. Oddo dropped the window frame back down with a soft thump.

Freddie's belly filled with butterflies as they waited for Mungo to let them in.

It took a moment for Mungo to undo the lock. The screen door slid open and they went through the kitchen, moving single file up the staircase.

Jordan was at the front. He waved the rest of them on with his left hand, holding his right index finger to his lips. They crept down the hallway. Freddie's slippered feet didn't make a sound.

Yapzilla sat comfortably in the upturned palms of Nina's hands. The double-necked monster let off a small but steady stream of fire to light their way.

They stopped before a door covered with insect stickers. "This must be Trevor's room," Jordan said.

"Thanks, Captain Obvious." Manny rolled his eyes.

"Manny, you be the lookout," Jordan went on.

"Why do I have to be lookout?" Manny asked.

"Chain of command, brother," Jordan replied.

Manny grumbled disapprovingly and stood outside Trevor's room with his arms crossed.

Oddo and Mungo stayed in the upstairs hall, with Manny on the lookout.

Nina then quietly pushed open Trevor's door. It

opened without a squeak. She walked in first, followed by Jordan, Quincy, and Freddie, who was walking softly in his bunny slippers.

On the other side of the room, Trevor slept on a twin bed. He lay flat on his stomach. His pajamas had little blue grasshoppers and orange butterflies checkered all over them. His bedspread and wallpaper were also covered with bugs and spiders and insects. It was bug heaven . . . if you were into that sort of thing. If you weren't, it was totally disgusting!

"Okay," Jordan said. "Let's do this."

The four of them split up to find the bug monsters. Nina tiptoed around on the other side of the room and scanned the bookcase and dresser.

Jordan looked under Trevor's bed. Freddie scanned the shelves, which held hundreds of jars and cases filled with various insects. Freddie got the willies just looking at the creepy-crawlies.

Come on, he thought to himself. *Find the printer, get the bugs, and then get outta here.* . . . Freddie tiptoed in his pink bunny slippers alongside Trevor's bed. He was

so close to Trevor he could almost feel the breeze from his snoring.

Suddenly, Trevor flipped over in his bed, kicking one of his pillows to the floor. They all held their breaths, praying silently that he would stay asleep.

On the other side of the bed, Jordan held Kraydon in the palm of his hand. The muscle-bound minimonster's eyeball rotated and he fired a pulse at Trevor's sleeping body. The snoring stopped as Trevor turned to stone.

Freddie shot a glare at Jordan and Kraydon.

"What?" Jordan said coyly. "We'll turn him back after we're done."

Then in the flickering glow of Yapzilla's fire breath, Freddie saw a familiar object underneath the nightstand.

It was the 3D printer . . . the same one that had been taken from Freddie's locker. There was only one package of 3D printing goo left.

"Got the printer," Freddie whispered.

"Nice work, big fella." Jordan gave him a thumbs-up.

"Good job, Freddie," Nina whispered from across the room.

Just then, Manny burst in the bedroom and shut the door softly.

"What are you doing?" Jordan asked. "You're supposed to be standing watch."

"Shhhh!" Manny said. "Trevor's mom's coming. . . . Everybody hide!"

Freddie and Manny hid under the bed. Nina slipped in the closet. Jordan ducked behind the chair in the corner. Quincy crouched under the desk.

Suddenly a voice sounded on the other side of the door. "Trevvy, are you still up?"

Freddie's eyes widened. Trevor was currently a stone statue! *Think, think, what did Trevor's voice sound like?* Freddie was terrible at impersonations, but he knew someone who wasn't. He nudged his oldest pal.

Manny swallowed hard and opened his mouth. "Yeah, Mom, sorry . . . I was just, uh, doing something . . . ," he said in a soft, nasally, higher-pitched voice.

Mrs. Kelso's voice sounded again through the door. "Okay, well, go back to bed, lamb chop."

"Sure thing, Mumsy. Nighty night."

Jordan nearly burst out laughing when Manny said the word *mumsy.*

They listened quietly as Trevor's mom's footsteps faded down the hallway.

Phew! Freddie thought. *That was a close one.*

Except their problems were far from over.

When Nina came out of the closet, she had a glassy-eyed look on her face.

"What's wrong, Nina?" Freddie asked.

"Guys . . . ," she said in a strange voice. "I found the

bugs." She passed a mason jar to Freddie. Inside, the two entomon bugs chittered and clacked against the glass.

Quincy opened the tin box of silica-filled slugs and fed them to the entomon bugs. The entomons gobbled up the slugs, swallowing the silica that made sure they stayed little.

"There," he said, putting the lid back on the jar. "Mission accomplished."

But Nina was still standing there in a trance.

"Nina, come on! We got the bugs and the printer! Let's get out of here," Freddie urged her, but Nina wasn't budging. She just stood with her back to them, facing the closet, mesmerized.

"What's the matter with her?" Manny asked as they all stepped closer.

Yapzilla's flaming snout cast a glow inside the closet.

The four boys looked in and gasped, holding their breaths, all trying not to scream.

The whole inside of the closet was coated with ripe, burbling egg sacs. The ento-eggs looked ready to burst. Some of the insects already had, and the baby entomons' legs and heads were starting to pop out.

"Yapzilla, torch 'em!" Jordan said.

"Are you crazy, man?" Freddie said, stopping Yapzilla. "We could burn the whole house down!"

"I'm with Freddie," Quincy said. "Too risky."

"There's got to be some other way," Manny said.

Then all of a sudden the egg sacs began to bulge and wiggle, bulge and jiggle more and more rapidly. "They're all going to hatch," Nina said, breaking her silence. "And

I think I just threw up in my mouth a little. . . ."

The entomons' offspring erupted from the bulging insect eggs and dropped from the ceiling, falling to the floor with a pitter-pat, patter-patter. The freshly hatched bugs crawled across the ceiling, down the walls. They were bigger than Freddie expected, and there were so many. Too many. Hundreds, if not more.

 Suddenly, the mason jar started to clink as the two original entomons scratched and tapped their claws against the glass. Then just as suddenly, the closet full of baby entomonsters fixed their attention on the five kids.

The original two entomons in the jar were going berserk. Freddie, Jordan, and Nina backed away from the door, as the bugs in the closet started to mobilize.

"Jordan, turn Trevor back and let's get the heck out of here!" Freddie whisper-yelled.

Kraydon quickly zapped Trevor back to life, and the kids left Trevor's bedroom as quickly and quietly as they possibly could. Freddie glanced back as the insect swarm skittered out of the closet like a puddle of oozing lava.

It was coming right for them.

"Come on!" Quincy said, and hurried down the stairs.

Manny gathered up the five minimonsters at the bottom of the staircase and put them in his backpack.

The kids picked up speed as they hit the first floor and hustled through the living room. Behind them, the bugs spiraled down the bannister and poured over the landing and down the staircase. Each of them was about the size of a fun-size Snickers bar. Except way less delicious.

All Freddie could think about was how much he did not want to die tonight.

The baby bug swarm swept across the family room, coating everything in squirming, scuttling insects.

The five kids hustled through the kitchen, and Jordan slid open the back door. He motioned for Freddie to go first, and Freddie slipped out into the backyard,

followed by Nina, Manny, Quincy, and Jordan, who pushed the screen door shut behind them.

As Freddie carried them across the lawn, the two bugs in the jar glowed on and off like a beacon.

"Why are they glowing like that?" Nina asked.

"Bioluminescence," Quincy said. "Like fireflies or plankton."

They heard a strange noise behind them, like metal ripping. The baby bugs sliced through the screen door.

"Go!" Freddie whispered to his friends urgently, and they all raced across the yard as the baby entomons chased after them.

"Why do they keep following us?" Quincy asked as they ran.

"Because they're freakin' bonkers . . . ," Manny said, as they hightailed it through the yard. His backpack full of monsters jostled and bounced.

Freddie stared at the glowing entomonsters inside the mason jar. "I think they're following us because we have their entomon parents."

"The parentomons . . . ," Nina said ominously, as they stopped near the fence at the end of the yard.

The kids watched the swarm of baby monster bugs in horror. The entomon offspring skittered out of Trevor's window and down the side of the house. In the dark, it looked like Trevor's room was overflowing with thick, black oil.

At that very moment something rustled around the cuff of Freddie's pants.

More entomon bugs raced around Freddie's feet, making him dance like his pants were on fire. He stumbled over his own two feet, twitching and flinching as something scuttled up the inside of his shirt. One of the baby bug monsters scurried up his armpit, tickling his skin.

"Look out, man!" Jordan warned Freddie as the kids backed away from him.

The swarm pooled around Freddie's feet.

"Ahhh!" Freddie muffled his mouth with his hand, trying to keep quiet.

The entomonster swarm scurried up his body, covering him all the way to his neck. Freddie flailed his arms and kicked his bunny-slippered feet. He tried to run away, but he lost his balance and tripped.

The mason jar went flying out of his hand and shattered on the concrete walkway.

The two glowing entomons scrambled out of the broken jar.

"Freddie, just leave them, let's go!" Quincy whisper-yelled.

The baby bugs headed straight for the escaped monster bugs.

The glowing parentomons hissed and lunged at Freddie with their pincers.

The entoswarm was about to reach its parent bugs, when Freddie lifted his big foot to squash them.

As he brought his pink bunny slipper down, someone tackled him from the side and sent him crashing to the ground.

It was Trevor. And he was furious.

"What do you think you're doing?!" Trevor cried as he got off the ground.

Freddie dusted himself off as he watched the swarm of entomons follow the parentomon bugs toward the plants at the edge of the yard. "What the heck was that for?"

"You never should have separated them from the brood!" Trevor whisper-shouted. "The offspring will do anything to stay with their parents. Now they're out in the world, you idiots!"

"Us idiots?" Nina said, then pointed at Trevor. "You idiot!"

"At least I know you can't just release a new species out into the wild all willy-nilly like!" Trevor said.

"I don't know who Willy or Nilly are," Jordan said, "but I'm pretty sure we're nothing like them!"

"Why did you make a bug monster in the first place?" Manny asked.

"*Insect* monster," Trevor corrected. "All bugs are insects, but not all insects are bugs. But to answer your question, I wanted to make a monster like you guys had made for yourselves."

"How did you know about our monsters?" Freddie asked in a panic.

Trevor looked shifty and didn't answer.

"But why insects?" Jordan continued.

"I love all insects," Trevor said. "They're my true friends."

"But why did you have to make two of them?" Freddie asked.

"I didn't," Trevor explained. "I only made the one, but then it turned into two."

"It did what?" Quincy asked.

"You should have seen it replicate," Trevor said. "It looked like something out of a horror movie... so awesome!"

"There's a wild pack of bug monsters loose in our town," Nina said. "And you think that's awesome?"

"Newsflash, bro," Jordan said. "Bugs that can reptile themselves are not in the awesome category."

"Replicate," Trevor corrected him.

"That's what I said." Jordan scowled. "Reptilicate themselves."

"Wait, you guys," said Freddie. "Something weird is happening!"

The entomons swarmed into a giant swirling mass, moving across the backyard, covering every surface like a thick black

48

shadow. They clung to every last shred of vegetation, munching and crunching as they fed on the grass, trees, and any type of roughage they could sink their razor-sharp mandibles into.

The kids watched as the swarm of entomons spiraled up a forty-foot pine tree, covering every inch of bark.

After a few swirls around the trunk, the swarm descended, and all that was left of the tree were bare, dead branches.

"What the freak!" Freddie exclaimed. "They just ate all the pine needles off the tree!"

The bug swarm spiraled up the next tree and did the same thing.

The entomons grazed through the second evergreen like someone

winning a corn-on-the-cob-eating contest.

"In case anyone was wondering," whispered Manny as he clutched the straps of his backpack, "this is not good."

Oddo and Mungo unzipped the zipper and peeked out their heads. They went wide-eyed as they took in the destruction. In a matter of minutes, every tree in sight was stripped bare by the swarm. And it wasn't just the trees. As the swarm ascended and descended the last pine tree in the backyard, Freddie heard a funny sound.

Actually, it wasn't funny at all.

Chicka-chicka-chicka. . . whoosh!

"Oh shoot!" Nina yelled. "The sprinklers!"

The Kelsos' automatic sprinklers popped out of the ground and sprayed the lawn, drenching the kids and the swarm, and soaking Manny's backpack.

"We have to get them out of here before they start growing!" Jordan said. "Charge!"

"Wait," Trevor said too late. "I don't think that's such a good idea."

But Jordan was already running at the bug swarm,

shooing them away from the sprinklers. The insects dispersed as he stomped toward them. The swarm converged back together and started to nip at Jordan's ankles.

"Change of plans!" Jordan yelled, sprinting back toward Freddie and the gang with the swarm at his heels. "Retreat!"

"You ticked them off, dummy!" Manny yelled.

The entomon horde surged at their heels like ocean surf at high tide.

Trevor ran over to the door of his garage and they

all followed. "Quick, everybody in here!" He held open the side door and Freddie hustled inside after Manny, Jordan, Nina, and Quincy.

The door clicked shut, keeping out the entomon swarm.

The garage smelled musty, like old stale wood. Trevor flicked a switch on the wall. They were lit with a dingy orange glow.

Freddie looked down at his feet. His bunny slippers were now soaking wet and covered in lime-green bug guts. Not only that, but they were shredded from the swarm of monstrous insects that had been clawing and nipping around his feet.

Outside, Freddie heard the pitter-patter of tiny ento-mon feet scrambling over the roof. He ran to the small window on the garage wall just in time to see the two glowing dots of the parentomons skittering off to find a new location and a new feast. Eventually, the monster bugs followed their parents and the infestation disap-peared into the night.

They were safe . . . at least for a second.

"Are those things going to grow now?" Manny asked. "Please tell me they're not going to grow."

"The silica should have already kicked in on the parentomons," said Nina.

"But not on their entospawn," Quincy said. "Which begs the question: Why in the world did you let them reproduce?"

"I didn't," Trevor said. "I let them chill out in the closet while I did my homework. I didn't think they were going to hatch a whole colony in the time it takes to do a few math problems."

Just then Manny's waterlogged backpack started rustling like crazy.

"Whoa!" Manny wriggled out of the shoulder straps and set the bag down. The fabric ripped as their minimonsters burst out and tumbled onto the floor.

Kraydon, Yapzilla, Mega-Q, Oddo, and Mungo looked exactly the same, but there was one major difference. The minimonsters weren't so mini anymore.

They were about as big as five large stuffed animals. Kraydon and Oddo were the biggest. Yapzilla was bigger than Mega-Q and Mungo, who were about the same size, except Mega-Q had grown to about the length of a dachshund.

"Um, why are our monsters bigger?" Freddie asked. "We gave them silica!"

Manny turned to Quincy. "Yeah, Mr. Know-It-All, how did they grow?"

"I don't know," Quincy said sheepishly. "It must have worn off?"

Oddo burped and grew even larger, right before their eyes. He shook his fur like a dog after a swim and water sprayed everywhere.

"We gotta make them small again, ASAP!" Nina said. "Who has the silica?"

"We could try...." Quincy pulled the silica slugs out of his pocket, ready to shrink them down.

"Hold up, guys!" Jordan, who had been nervously tugging at his thick dark hair, said. "What's so bad about having big monsters if we also have big bugs?"

"Wait a minute," Trevor said. "Are you saying the entomons are going to get as big as these guys, too?"

"It depends," Nina said, "on how much water they absorbed." Yapzilla stretched out her neck and it grew some more. "If it's as much water as these guys, we could be in even *bigger* trouble."

Trevor scratched his scalp, lost in thought. "I knew I shouldn't have added in the locust with everything else.

I just couldn't resist," Trevor said.

"What is it about the locusts?" Quincy asked.

Trevor glanced up. "The desert locust can consume its own weight in food every day."

"Is that bad?" asked Nina.

"It's not," said Trevor, "when they weigh less than an ounce. . . ."

"But who knows how big these bugs are gonna get now . . . ," said Quincy. "This could mean an ecological collapse on a global scale."

"You're right!" Trevor said, turning to the rest of them. "He's right."

"Quincy's well aware," Nina said. "You don't need to tell him."

"Well, if they're feeding, then now would be a good time for us to attack with our big monsters," Trevor said.

"Come on, you guys," Freddie said. "Let's gear up. . . ."

They started to look around the garage, rummaging through everything.

The place was a real mess. There were piles upon piles of clutter and junk: boxes and clothes and tools and jars and nets and old moldy aquariums and terrariums and ant farms, an unopened economy pack of bug poison.

There were all kinds of sports equipment as well, practically brand-new. It was strange. Trevor didn't strike Freddie as the athletic type.

"Why do you have all this stuff?" Manny asked.

"Before the bugs," Trevor said, "my parents were trying to get me involved in activities. . . . Nothing really took."

"Wait a second," Quincy said, picking something out of a grungy old cardboard box. "I knew you looked familiar." He held up a patch for Northwest Horizons science camp. "You went to my science camp two years ago!"

"I did! That place was rad!" Trevor said. "Did you hear the rumors about the aliens there?"

"Those are just rumors," Quincy said confidently. "Nothing more than a hoax."

"Guys, can we stay focused—" Freddie started to say when Jordan interrupted, holding up a practice jersey for a soccer team.

"And you tried out for my soccer team," Jordan said.

"You were awful!"

Trevor looked a little hurt. "You could have passed me the ball at least once. . . ."

"Why would I have done that? I was trying to win."

Trevor ignored Jordan and turned to Nina. "And I tried out for a play you starred in."

"I thought you looked familiar," she said. "So you knew who we were?"

"When I saw you guys on the news after the monster attack, I recognized the three of you. I started to follow you. Freddie and Manny didn't seem like the types you three would hang with, and you all had cool little monster friends, so I pieced it together. The monsters. The 3D printer. Freddie's drawings. I heard everything. You know you should probably be more careful about making sure nobody's spying on you."

"So why didn't you just ask us about it instead of sneaking around behind our backs?" Freddie asked.

"I didn't think you'd hang out with me unless I had a monster of my own." Trevor looked sad as he admitted the truth. "I'm sorry."

"Well, we're going to need you to solemnly pinky swear that you will never, ever tell anyone about the monsters." Manny stuck out his pinky and Trevor hooked his finger. "And that you'll help us stop these monster bugs, even if it means squishing every last one of them."

Trevor let out a long sigh. "And I know these bugs need to be contained, but you have to understand, as scary as you guys think they are and as much destruction as they'll cause, deep down, I love them. . . ."

Freddie crinkled his eyebrows, but he understood. He would feel the same way about his monsters. Even though Trevor's monsters were way more disgusting and way less lovable than his.

"You have to pinky swear that you're on our side," Manny said.

"I swear it."

"And promise that you'll never tell anyone what you know."

"Who would I tell?"

"Your friends."

"I don't have those."

"Just swear you won't tell anyone."

"I pinky swear."

"All right, Trevor, welcome to the team," Freddie said. "Now let's grab what we need and go get these suckers."

Jordan tossed Freddie a lacrosse stick and kept one for himself. Manny found two cans of Raid bug killer and Nina unearthed the spray cans of bug repellent. Each of them grabbed a street hockey stick. Quincy picked up two tennis rackets, and Trevor snagged a double-sided

oar from a camping trip. Freddie slipped off his disgusting slime-soaked slippers and borrowed a pair of work boots.

Manny found a gallon of bottled water and lugged it outside. He whistled and their not-so-mini monsters gathered around. Oddo and Kraydon had both grown past Manny's hips. Yapzilla's necks hit just under Manny's chin, and Mungo and Mega-Q both came halfway up his shins. He was about to dump the gallon of water over the five of them when Freddie interrupted.

"Don't make them too big," he said. "After all, bigger isn't always better." He knew that better than anyone.

"Quit worrying, man," Manny said. "Don't you trust me?"

"Of course I trust you," Freddie said.

"Then act like it." Manny poured out the gallon jug and doused their monsters with water.

After a few moments, the monsters grew again. Kraydon's body inflated to the size of a boulder as he grew to the height of Freddie's shoulder. Mega-Q's body thickened to the girth of a corgi and lengthened to the dimensions of a large snake. Oddo and Yapzilla tripled in size, and Mungo got about as big as a chimpanzee.

"Now they can do some serious damage," Manny said with a grin, and patted Mungo on his head.

7

The kids crept into the night and sneaked down the side of the Kelsos' garage. They followed Trevor through the neighbor's yard, their freshly grown monsters in tow.

"Where are we going?" Freddie asked.

"We're heading for the park," Trevor said.

"How do we know they're there?" asked Quincy.

"They'll stick together in a pack, going after areas of heavy vegetation," Trevor said. "That means they're probably at the park now. It's close—we'll be there in a couple minutes."

The town park didn't look like the rest of their southwestern desert town. It had grass and trees and flowers and bushes. They slowed down as they approached the gate. A buzzing noise filled the air as the entomons chewed on the trees and munched on the grass. It was one of the creepiest sounds Freddie had ever heard.

Silently, they opened the gate and looked for a place to hide. Oddo and Kraydon barely fit behind a grazed-down tree, but the rest of them lurked in the shadows and gazed upon the swarm.

The average size of the entomons had doubled. The bug monsters now ranged from as small as a mouse to as big as a full-grown dog.

Freddie watched as one of the monstrous insects rippled and bulged in a frighteningly quick growth

spurt. In a matter of seconds, the entomon bug went from the size of a guinea pig to that of a pit bull.

"That is so not freakin' cool," Jordan said.

"You guys," Nina said. "I don't know about this. . . ."

"They're only going to get bigger. Let's go!" Jordan said, crouching like a big cat ready to pounce. Kraydon smashed his giant claws together.

"We have to be smarter than them," Manny said, holding Jordan back. "We can't just charge in on them."

"Why not?!" Jordan said, getting himself pumped up. "We got Raid and nets and weapons and bigger monsters. We're rollin' deep, baby! It's battle time. Woo!"

"Shhhh!" They all shushed the gung ho superjock.

"Manny's right," said Nina. "We have to be strategic if we're going to stand a chance." Together, they laid out a plan. The monsters nodded along in agreement.

Including monsters, they were a team of eleven. If they all worked as a team, they just might be able to take the entomon swarm.

"Get as many as you can as fast as possible," Trevor whispered. "As soon as they feel threatened, they'll stop eating and protect their food supply. . . ."

Jordan crept out in front of them like a guerrilla warrior. The rest of them spread out to the edge of the infested park.

"On the count of three," Freddie whispered. "One, two—"

"*Yum yums!*" Mungo screamed as he ran toward the bugs. The rest of the big monsters raced after him.

"Three . . . ," Freddie said, and looked at Manny, who shrugged.

"They're monsters. What do you expect?"

"Go!" Nina yelled, and they charged into the bug-filled park.

The monsters galloped out in front of the kids.

Kraydon shot his giant eye beam, turning a slew of entomons to stone, then smashed them all with his spiked tail. Anything in the pulsating cylinder of Kraydon's one-eyed gaze turned to stone. The muscle-bound brute could take out twenty or so entomons in one shot, but there were thousands upon thousands of these things covering the park.

Mega-Q shot electric blue sparks at the insects, like a real-life bug zapper.

Yapzilla spewed a humongous swath of fire, torching a giant bug that was even bigger than Kraydon.

Oddo jumped furiously from bug to bug, squishing as many of them as he could with all three arms and both his legs. The monster bugs made a sickening

crunch as they exploded onto his fur. Bright green goo spurted from their ruptured guts.

Mungo zipped around, chowing down on a bug feast. "Yum yums!" he said happily between munches.

"Ewww, Mungo, stop that!" said Manny, as he hit a trio of jumbo entomons with a slap shot from his hockey stick.

Jordan scooped up a lacrosse stick full of smaller entomons and flung them against the cement walkway. Freddie stamped his boots and squashed them with squishy crunch after squishy crunch.

"Take that!" Nina brought her hockey stick over her head and swatted a bunch off the swing set.

Trevor delicately squished one bug at a time, a pained look on his face. "Sorry," he whispered with each smush.

Even though they were crushing dozens at a time, the swarm seemed endless.

"How many of these things are there?" Quincy sighed, kicking slime off his cowboy boots and swatting at the bugs with his tennis rackets. "The more I squash, the more there are!"

Freddie swiped at a swarm of granola bar–size entomons with his lacrosse stick as they crawled up his legs,
rising to his waist. He hit them off as fast as he could,
but they kept coming and coming, one after another.
There were so many he could barely see straight. "Keep
fighting!" Freddie mumbled, trying not to get any bugs
in his mouth.

Quincy swung his racket like a giant fly swatter and
caught a dozen entomonsters with a hard backhand.

Pock! Pock! Pock! Pock!

Psssst! Manny sprayed the Raid around his ankles as
the bug monsters tried to scurry up his legs. Ten yards
to his left, Jordan swung madly with the lacrosse stick,
like a medieval swordsman fighting the battle of his life.

To his right, Nina was spinning in a cloud of bug
spray so thick that Freddie lost sight of her. Out of the
chemical cloud he heard her shriek and watched as an
enormous entomon tackled her to the ground.

Freddie raced across the bug-coated grass as the
massive entomonster reared back, about to slice Nina's
arms with its razor-sharp pincers.

Freddie rammed the end of the lacrosse stick into

the monster bug's face and felt a satisfying squish.

The monster bug shrieked, black pus shooting out of its eyehole, as Freddie pulled Nina up off the ground.

While the kids stomped and swatted and bashed the skittering carpet of monster bugs, their monsters kept the larger insects at bay. Oddo drop-kicked a massive entomon, crushing its body with his large monster heel, while Mungo ran circles around one bug as big as a Labrador before smashing its noggin with a swift karate chop.

The massive bug creatures growled and grunted, more like large mammals than insects. An entomon as large as a rottweiler charged at Nina. Just in time, Yapzilla scorched the big bug with a stream of fire. The

bug screeched and flipped on its back. Its legs squiggled in the air until Kraydon blasted the upside-down bug monster with his eye beam and the thing hardened to stone.

Mega-Q zapped three Chihuahua-size entomons as they charged behind Quincy.

"There's too many of them!" Nina yelled, and they sprinted away from the roiling cluster of psychotic insects.

Then suddenly, the bugs started to empty out of the park.

The kids stopped fighting, panting in the cool night air.

"What's going on?" Freddie asked.

"They're retreating!" Jordan said.

"Thank goodness!" Nina exhaled. "'Cuz. That. Was. Disgusting."

"I don't think they're retreating...," Trevor observed. "I think they're moving on to their next meal."

They all looked around.

The entire park was completely bare. The gigantic bugs had eaten everything in sight and they were only just getting warmed up.

Freddie was still in shock. They'd squashed hundreds of bugs and they hadn't even made a dent in the entoswarm.

Manny's eyes darted left to right. "Which way do you think they went?"

"What about the cornfields off the highway?" Quincy said.

"If I were an entomon," Trevor said, "that's where I'd be."

"Then that's where we're going," Freddie said.

All eleven of them rushed out of the park and paused at the side of a road—Freddie, Manny, Jordan, Nina, Quincy, Oddo, Mungo, Kraydon, Yapzilla, Mega-Q, and Trevor. Freddie's eyes strained through the darkness, trying to spot the bugs. He'd never been outside this late before.

Everything was silent except for the constant chirp of desert crickets and the wind whipping through the night. The town was much less populated since the monster madness two weeks ago. A lot of people had left town during the monster attack, and most of them hadn't returned. They were scared that the monsters were going to come back. Freddie glanced up at Oddo, who was now taller than Freddie. *They weren't wrong*, he thought.

It wasn't too far down the road when they crossed a set of railroad tracks. A minute or two later they found themselves at the edge of the interstate.

On the other side of the four-lane roadway, they came upon a stretch of farmland, eight square acres of cornfield.

"I don't see anything," Manny said, scanning the landscape.

Oddo sniffed the air, walking forward as if he had just caught a scent. They followed the fluffy monster down the deserted highway.

In the distance, Freddie could make out a strange blue light.

"There they are!" he exclaimed, and started to jog toward the glow.

They watched as the swarm glided toward the field and began to feast on the farmland. It sounded like a band saw cutting through a thick piece of wood.

The entomons were chowing down, devouring the corn at an alarming rate. Some of the bigger ones were eating whole corn stalks in a single bite.

It looked like there were even more of them than before.

"How is that even possible?" Nina asked, sounding a little freaked out.

Even in the darkness, Freddie could see Trevor's face going completely white.

"They must be replicating. . . ." Trevor's voice trailed off.

"How do you know that?" Jordan asked.

"The first one split into two after I fed it," said Trevor. "So the more they eat, the more they replicate."

"Look!" Manny pointed, droop-jawed.

Freddie squinted and made out the shape of one gigantic entomon. As the monster bug consumed the cornstalk, its middle started to bulge as it divided into two identical entomons.

"We need a different plan, you guys," said Freddie. "We can't kill all these bugs with a couple tennis rackets and a few cans of bug spray."

Quincy scratched his head, thinking hard. "We know they are drawn to the original two entomons, so maybe we can lure them somewhere if we kidnap the two parents."

"I've got it," Manny blurted out. "*Night of the Lepus!*"

"What's that?" Nina asked.

"*Lepus* is Latin for *bunny rabbit*," Quincy replied.

Manny turned to Freddie. "*Night of the* freaking

Lepus, dude. Do you remember we watched it, like, a month ago at my house?"

"Of course, I remember. You don't exactly forget a movie about giant killer bunnies terrorizing a small Texas town." Freddie gave his best friend a grin.

"Do you remember the end?" Manny said.

Freddie thought for a moment. "The railroad tracks!"

"Yep, they electrified them and ran all the giant killer bunnies across them."

"Spoiler alert! I would have watched that," Nina said. "I love old horror movies!"

Jordan looked at them both funny. "How are we going to electrify the train tracks?"

"Mega-Q!" Manny and Freddie yelled at the same time, and they both did a happy little jig, dancing around in a circle. To Freddie, it felt just like old times with Manny.

"Wow, they are, like, really nerding out right now," Trevor said to Nina.

"Their nerdiness may just help us get out of this mess," Nina said.

"Okay, you guys, here's the plan," Manny announced.

"We're going to lure the parentomons out of the pack and to the train tracks."

"Which Mega-Q will have to electrify," clarified Freddie. "But first, we need a way to get those two glowing creepy-crawlies out of the middle of that field."

Oddo and Mungo had been listening intently. In a flash they jumped into action.

They thundered across the highway and paused for a moment on the brink of the infested cornfield. Oddo wrapped Mungo in a three-armed bear hug and curled up into a round mound of fur.

The green fluffball rolled forward and disappeared into the base of the corn stalks. Oddo and Mungo headed toward the center of the feeding frenzy, where the parentomons' glow dimmed and brightened, pulsing at the heart of the swarm.

Freddie squinted through the darkness, but he couldn't make out what was happening.

"What's going on?" Manny said nervously.

"They shouldn't have gone in there," Trevor said. "That swarm could chew them up and spit them out in, like, two seconds."

"Thank you for that, Trevor," Nina said. "Now if you could please shut up for the remainder of forever, that would be fantastic."

"Don't worry," Manny said. "Mungo's too quick for them."

"And he's got Oddo to help protect him."

Out in the middle of the cornfield, there was a flurry of movement. Mungo appeared back on the empty highway with the glowing blue bugs under his arms. Mungo sped toward them with Oddo trailing behind, galloping on all fives like a gorilla.

"They made it!" Quincy cheered as the roar of the feeding swarm swelled.

"Come on," Freddie said. "To the train tracks!"

The kids raced toward the railroad tracks, cutting across the other side of the highway. "Go on, Mega," Quincy said. "Do your thing."

Mega-Q crawled up the electric pole and sent a surge through the tracks. The metal tracks hummed and buzzed with electric current.

Down the road, Mungo was heading right toward them. Oddo galloped after him, the swarm close behind him. It looked like a stampede of beasts escaped from a zoo. But not a normal zoo, a zoo for alien insects. Most of the bugs were at least the size of full-grown felines, with some as big as baby rhinos.

"Go, Mungo!" Jordan hooted.

"Come on, Oddo!" Nina hollered.

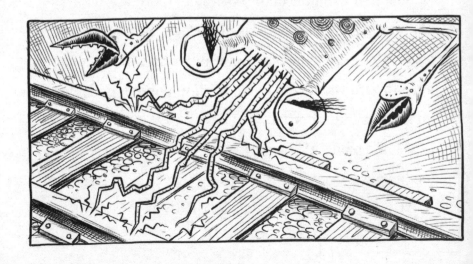

Their two monsters hopped over the electrified tracks and stood on the other side with the parentomonster bugs.

As the massive swarm of grotesque insects crossed the railroad, the bugs snapped and sizzled, dropping on the electrified tracks.

"It's working, it's working!" Trevor yelled.

Just then Mungo yelped and fumbled the two glowing ringleader bugs. The parentomons broke free from Mungo's grasp.

"Oh no!" Manny cried, as Mungo hit the ground.

The parentomons escaped his clutches and scuttled toward the tracks. It looked like they were going to stop, as if they knew to not electrocute themselves. Instead,

the bugs leaped into the air, fluttered for a moment, then landed on the other side of their swarm.

The swarm quickly scurried back into the field and got back to munching on corn.

Freddie elbowed Trevor in the side. "Did you just see that?" he asked in shock.

"They flew," Quincy said. "Well sort of, but they grew wings."

"Does that mean the rest of them will get wings, too?" Jordan asked.

"When they mature," Trevor said. "Yes."

"And then they'll all be able to fly?" Nina asked.

Trevor cringed. "Maybe?"

Over by the train tracks, Mungo howled in pain.

Nina and Manny rushed over to Mungo, who held his arm like it was in a sling.

The parentomons had clamped down on his fuzzy monster skin with their clawlike jaws, which was what had made him drop them.

Freddie was too shocked by what had just happened to think straight.

The parentomons had sprouted *wings*. Soon the rest of the entomons would be flying. But when?

The original two bugs were printed yesterday. And the swarm had hatched a few hours ago. That meant they had less than half a day before the whole swarm took flight.

Freddie tried to picture the rhino-size entomon flying around in the air and felt sick. He was covered in bug slime and the fight seemed far from over. His entire town was about to be eaten by flying bugs. And if he didn't stop them, they'd move to the next town and the next, and soon the whole world would be consumed.

Nina and Manny helped Mungo as he limped back to the group.

"Strike one," Trevor said. "What do we do now?"

"They hurt my Mungo, and now they're gonna pay. Let's exterminate these suckers," Manny said.

"But we're almost out of this stuff!" Jordan said, shaking a Raid can.

"I'm not talking about Raid. We need the real deal!" said Manny.

"How are we going to do that?" asked Quincy.

"My uncle's extermination company is down the road," Manny said, brushing Mungo off. "Let's roll."

Oddo curled up into a fluffball and started to roll out ahead of them.

"It's just a figure of speech, dude . . . ," Manny yelled after him, but Oddo was already leading the way.

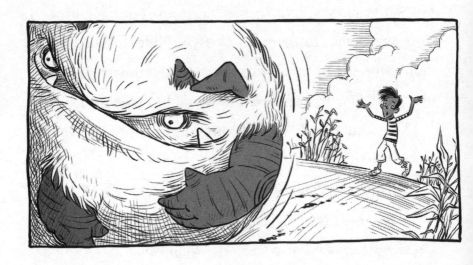

The group reached the warehouse about ten minutes later, hearts pounding, lungs heaving. In the driveway was a truck with Vasquez Pest Control written on the side.

The skeleton of a bare pine tree loomed over the building. The land had already been picked clean by the entomon swarm.

"Are these things just going to keep eating until there're no plants left?" Nina asked Trevor.

"I think so. But that's not the worst part," Trevor said, looking sheepish.

"What could be worse than that?" Manny asked.

"Well, there's something I haven't told you guys yet. . . ."

Freddie looked at him. "What is it?"

"These bugs are *polyphagous*," Trevor said, as if this were the most basic word in the English language.

"What the heck does that mean?" asked Jordan.

"It means that they're herbivores," Quincy said. "But they could become carnivores!"

"English, please?" said Jordan.

"Once they run out of plants, they'll start to eat animals," Trevor said. "And once they run out of animals . . ."

Freddie gulped. "Humans?"

Trevor nodded. "Sorry?"

"You're killing us, Trevor!" Nina said.

"Why would you design them to do that?"

"It seemed cool at the time," Trevor said. "Obviously, I didn't think it through."

"Ugh. Come on, let's get what we need and get outta there," Manny said. "We don't have a second to lose."

Mega-Q zapped out the alarm system, and Kraydon smashed the locked door handle and the door swung open.

"Your uncle's gonna be mad!" said Freddie, looking at the busted door.

"What else are we supposed to do?" Manny said. "He'll have to understand."

Inside the warehouse, there were storage shelves all the way to the ceiling. They were stacked with metal tanks of industrial-strength bug-killing chemicals.

They read: Keep Away from Open Flame! Highly Flammable!

The kids grabbed the extermination gear and hoisted the metal tanks over their shoulders like backpacks. Oddo, Kraydon, and Yapzilla carried two extra tanks apiece and followed the kids. They hustled out of the warehouse and darted back into the bug-infested night.

Back at the cornfield, the sound of the feeding frenzy filled the air. The kids split up and began to cover the field's perimeter with the toxic chemicals. The ento-mons ignored them. They were too busy eating and multiplying.

"It's not working!" Nina shouted.

"Just give it a minute," Manny said. "My uncle says they use the strongest stuff on the market."

"Well, your uncle never had to exterminate giant bug monsters from the deranged imagination of some psychotic sixth grader!" Quincy said, spraying another round of insecticide.

"I'm not psychotic!" Trevor replied. "I'm just misun-derstood."

Nina looked over at Yapzilla. "Are you thinking what I'm thinking?"

Yapzilla nodded with a sly smile.

"You want us to set everything on fire?" Trevor asked her.

"Good thinking, Nina!" Jordan said.

Quickly, they doused the rest of the field with the spray, and Yapzilla, now the size of an ostrich, reared back and unleashed a torrent of flames. The fire hit the insecticide, and the whole field went up in a blaze.

Pop! Pop! Pop!

The kids ducked for cover in a roadside ditch as the cornfield burst with popcorn.

The bugs were right in the thick of the fire. A high-pitched insectile screech pierced the air as the entomons burned and sizzled.

Pop! Pop! Pop!

Freddie could hear their guts exploding and bursting into the air. It was gross, but it was also pretty cool.

"Woo-hoo." Jordan high-fived Freddie. "We got 'em!"

Freddie relaxed, hoping this horrible

 night was over. But then, he noticed a great black wall rising through the flames. Within seconds, bugs of all sizes raced toward them, trying to escape the heat of the popcorn cornfield.

There were big ones and small ones, medium ones and tiny ones. The little entomons crackled and popped in the heat, but the bigger ones tore through the flames, screeching as they ran out of the fire, unscathed.

"Retreat!" Jordan shouted and took off for the road.

The kids and the monsters ran for their lives. The faster Freddie ran, the more the entomonsters gained on him.

"Someone do something!" Freddie yelled. "Help!

But it was too late.

They were bug meat for sure.

Freddie was way in last place, a good ten yards behind the rest of the gang. Yapzilla dropped back and trotted alongside him. The two-necked creature squawked, and Freddie plugged his ears as he ran. Yapzilla let out a high-pitched ear-piercing shriek right at the gaining swarm. The monster bugs stopped in their tracks, disoriented.

"Yo, nice trick, Yap!" Freddie cried, and sprinted as fast as he could.

Freddie caught up to his friends and they ducked into a red barn, shutting the doors behind them.

"It's not going to hold them!" Freddie shouted as the bugs buzzed closer.

Manny screamed back. "It's going to have to!"

Oddo braced the doors with his tripod of strong furry arms.

Squabam! The entomon swarm slammed into the barn. The hinges rattled and the doors shook. Oddo pushed against the wave of insects with all his might. A few bugs squeezed through the crack under the doors.

"They're getting in!" Freddie yelled, stomping and squashing and swatting at them with a stick.

Kraydon, who was now as tall as Freddie, roared and

pushed Oddo out of the way. He stood in the doorway and unleashed the rotating pulse from his Cyclops eye. The pulse struck the skittering critters around their feet as they squirmed through the gap between the doors and the dirt floor. The bugs turned to stone, and the kids smashed them.

But the bugs kept coming.

"There's too many for him to handle!" Manny yelled.

"If we had some kind of prism, we could refract Kraydon's eye beam and take out more of them at once," Quincy thought aloud. "Then he could cover more area with the pulse."

"I have this ring with my birthstone," Nina said, and passed it to Quincy.

"I've got this magnifying glass," Trevor said, handing it over.

"Good thinking, Quince," Freddie said, squashing an entomon the size of a loaf of bread.

"Hold them off as long as you can," Quincy said, and set to work, rigging the magnification lens and gemstone to put over Kraydon's eye.

The barn doors shook and rattled. The entomons funneled under the door in a steady stream.

"Everybody, get as many as you can," Manny shouted.

Oddo, Mungo, and Kraydon kept fighting. Oddo's fur was matted with green slime from body-slamming bug after bug like a pro wrestler. Mungo was doin' some serious kung-fuin', karate-chopping them to pieces. Kraydon turned the evil little pests to stone with his eye beam and clubbed them to smithereens.

A few seconds later, Quincy set the gemstone-magnifier on Kraydon's head. "Everyone, stand back!"

Kraydon's eye beam shot through the prism and refracted onto the oncoming swarm. The entire flock of bugs coming under the door turned to stone.

"Good job, Kraydon!" They all cheered, but another wave of insect monsters quickly followed. Kraydon's eye swirled again, turning them to stone, wave after wave until the stone-hardened bugs piled up, blocking the crack.

But Kraydon was running out of steam. His spiraling eyeball stopped rotating and slowed to a halt.

The barn doors started to rumble and rattle and *bam!* In a burst of splintered wood, the biggest entomon they'd seen yet crashed through the barn doors.

Screeeek! It squealed like a massive prize-winning hog as it ripped through the wood with its giant spiked beetle snout.

"Here they come!" Nina shouted as it tore a hole in the door.

The ginormous entomon tumbled inside the barn. A wave of entomons followed, their mandibles twitching, snapping, and snarling. They charged at the kids.

"Run!" Freddie shouted, and they ran for a ladder that climbed to the rafters of the barn. Oddo and Yapzilla scaled the ladder awkwardly, and Kraydon left a busted rung as he scrambled up to the wooden overhang.

Freddie and Jordan pried open the loft window while everyone else tipped bales of hay off the ledge of the hayloft, trying to crush the giant entomon. The big squares of hay slammed down onto the amassing pool of all-consuming insects with a bunch of crunchy splats.

Freddie peered out the window.

There were entomonsters skittering and crawling everywhere, as far as the eye could see. Moonlight reflected off their shiny beetle shells like a shimmering black lake.

Back inside, the entomon swarm scurried up the rungs of the ladder. Trevor pushed the bug-covered ladder away from the ledge and it fell to the floor.

It looked like they were trapped. But suddenly Freddie spotted a pickup truck parked next to the barn. The back was filled with hay.

That gave Freddie an idea.

"Come on—we have to jump!" Freddie said.

"We can't jump that far!" Nina said looking down. "This isn't the movies, Freddie."

Just then, Kraydon smashed a massive hole in upper wall of the barn. The monsters jumped down first and cleared the ground of any entomons.

One after the other, the kids dropped into the fluffy cushion of Oddo's arms. Kraydon and Yapzilla tossed the hay bales off the back of the pickup. Jordan and Nina hopped off and got into the front seats, Jordan on the driver's side. Freddie, Manny, Nina, Quincy, and Trevor crowded in the back with Oddo, Yapzilla, and Mungo.

"Start the engine!" Trevor howled, knocking off a slew of entomonsters from the side of the truck. "Hurry! There's more coming!"

Mega-Q curled himself up and squeezed between Nina and Jordan in the front, and Kraydon clung to the top of the cabin on all fours.

"Go, go, go!" Manny screamed next to Freddie's ear so loud, he nearly burst his eardrum.

But the keys weren't in the ignition.

"Mega-Q!" Quincy shouted up to his monster in the front seat. "Start the engine!"

The monster's eyeballs lit up, and Mega-Q jabbed one of his sharp legs into the ignition. The monster unleashed a surge of blue electricity, and the truck's engine started to purr.

"Good work, Mega!" Nina shouted and high-fived the monster. His neon-blue voltage shocked her hand. "Ow!"

The tires squealed and kicked up dirt and entomon guts as they tore onto the road. As they drove off, there was a loud thump behind them. Freddie whipped his head around.

"What was that?!" Freddie yelled.

The biggest bug monster yet, as big as a baby hippo, latched on to the back bumper.

"What's the matter back there?" Jordan hollered from the driver's seat. He slammed the gas, but the truck was anchored by the massive entomon.

"Shake it loose, shake it loose!" Freddie cried. "Side to side!"

The bumper sagged toward the monster bug's snout.

"Hang on!" Jordan switched gears and the engine revved. He jerked the wheel back and forth as they swerved through the charred cornfield.

The giant entomonster swung rapidly from side to side. The monster's toothy grip only tightened. They hit a bump at the edge of the road and the entomon flew back, ripping off the entire bumper. But at least they were finally free.

The truck's wheels spun, kicking up scorched popcorn. Mungo's tongue shot out of his mouth.

"Yum yums!" he cried gleefully into the night.

The pickup truck sped off down the highway, heading back into town.

As they jostled down the bumpy road, Freddie knew they needed a new plan. Their monsters were bigger and tougher now, but even they couldn't handle this swarm.

Freddie looked at his friends in the back of the pickup truck. They all looked back at Freddie. He knew what they were thinking.

"You know what we have to do, bro," Jordan called back, keeping his eyes on the road as he drove.

Freddie did know: they needed a bug-eating super monster. "All right," he said. "But this is the last monster we make. Ever."

"I'm cool with that," Manny said.

"Me, too," said Nina.

"Me three," Jordan said.

Quincy didn't say anything.

"What about you, Quincy?" Freddie said. "This needs to be unanimous."

"I mean, I guess so, unless we really need another one, right?"

Freddie glared at him.

"Okay, fine, no more monsters after this one, whatever . . . ," Quincy said.

Trevor huddled in the corner of the pickup truck, clutching his knees, eyes bugging out as he stared off into the New Mexico night.

"No more monsters," he whispered. "No more monsters . . ."

11

Now that they had the 3D printer, which Oddo was carrying in his extra hand, they decided to take it to Quincy's house. His parents were out of town. "They left you home alone?" Freddie asked.

"Nah," said Quincy. "My grandma's 'babysitting.' But it's cool."

"Your grandma's gonna be cool with five monsters in the house while we make another monster to defeat all the bug monsters that Trevor created?"

"No, she would totally not be cool with that," said Quincy. "But she's got an all-night poker game going with her friends at the retirement village. My parents don't know she's not home. It's our secret."

They whizzed down a back road. The sky was still dark. "Next left," Quincy said. "Right up there." They passed a water tower in the middle of a dirt lot. The words *Go 'Dillos!* were written on the side.

Moments later, Jordan pulled into the driveway of Quincy's house, and they quickly hustled their monsters inside.

"Grandma?" Quincy called out softly. When no one answered, he nodded. "Just checking . . . ," he whispered and motioned them all down into the basement.

Jordan and Nina yawned at the same time, their eyelids starting to droop. Trevor and Quincy looked exhausted, too. Freddie and Manny were both used to pulling all-nighters during video game marathons, so neither of them was feeling the effects of staying up so late. *It's like we are in our own video game,* Freddie thought. *Except there are no do-overs in this game of monsters. This one is life-and-death.*

"There's gummi candies in there." Quincy pointed to a cabinet next to the washing machine.

Freddie poured two large bags of gummi candy into a bowl, and their monsters ate off the floor of Quincy's basement, polishing off the bowl in less than a minute.

Jordan lugged the 3D printer over to a worktable, and Nina plugged it into the outlet on the wall. Manny set up the printer while Quincy hooked it up to his computer.

Freddie found a pad of paper and a few pencils from the storage closet.

They gathered around the monster-making worksta-
tion, looking over Freddie's shoulders.

"All right, guys and girl," Freddie said. "We need to
brainstorm."

Freddie rubbed his hands together, then cupped
them over his mouth and blew into them three times. It
was his way of getting ready to draw something supercool.

"It's gotta have a huge stomach," Quincy said. "Like
a bottomless pit so it won't stop eating."

Freddie drew a big oval in the center of the page.

"Good," Trevor said. "But more like an anteater."

"Anteater," Quincy said. "That's not a bad idea."

"Not an anteater though . . . ," said Manny. "An ENT-
eater . . ."

"And it's going to need more than one aardvark
snout if it's going to suck up all the entomons that are
out there . . . ," Nina added.

"What if it just had a really big snout, like an elephant's trunk?" Jordan said.

"Why can't it have more than one snout?" Manny

asked. "It can be whatever we want. We're the ones designing this thing."

"I don't know," Nina said. "More than one nose might look weird."

"Who cares if it looks weird?" Manny said. "As long as it gets the job done."

"I mean, I kind of care what it looks like," Trevor said. "This is going to be my monster."

"Wrong. Your monster is the disgusting little psycho bug that's out there reproducing into billions of other disgusting psycho bugs," said Nina.

"But you guys already have your own monsters. I'm the only one who doesn't." He sounded sad.

"That's because your monster turned into fifty bajillion monsters."

"I'm so sorry . . . ," Trevor blubbered.

Jordan looked over at him. "Dude, are you crying?"

"I'm not." Trevor rubbed his eyes with both hands.

"Because this is a no-crying zone," Jordan said.

"I'm not crying," Trevor said. "I just had something in my eye."

"Yeah," Jordan said. "Tears."

"Stop." Trevor reached out and punched Jordan in the shoulder.

Jordan looked at his shoulder, then stared at Trevor. "Just this once I'm going to let that slide."

"Can we please get back to our monster-eating monster?" Freddie pleaded, and they all focused back on the task at hand.

"Nina might be right about the snouts," said Quincy, getting them back on track. "It needs more range of motion than that. More like a bunch of arms that act like aardvark snouts."

"Guys, I think I've got it," Freddie interrupted. "We'll design it like an octopus, except the tentacles will slurp up the insects like an aardvark and be as big as elephant trunks. Its stomach will be able to digest as many entomons as it can eat. And it will still be strong enough to squash the entomons that have gotten too big to slurp."

Everyone stopped talking for a minute. They liked the sound of that.

"An octopus with tentacles like aardvark snouts as big as elephant trunks?" Quincy summarized.

"Sounds cool," Nina said.

"I can dig it." Jordan nodded.

"An octovarkephant," Manny said conclusively.

"Exactly," Freddie said, cracking his knuckles. He picked up a pencil and began to draw.

Jordan, Nina, Quincy, and Trevor crowded around him, looking over his shoulder.

Freddie's tongue hung out of the side of his mouth.

His eyes were laser focused.

"Give him some room," Manny said. "You can't crowd him while he's in the zone."

"It's all right," Jordan said. "He doesn't even know we're here."

"Yes, he does," said Manny. "You don't know him like I do."

"All right, chill out . . . ," Jordan said, backing off. "Sheesh, did he say no or something?"

Manny gave him a confused look. "Huh?"

"When you asked Freddie to marry you . . . ," Jordan said. "Did he turn you down or something?"

"Why don't you just hush, man!" Manny shouted.

"Shhhh!" Quincy shushed. "Both of you."

"Guys, relax!" Freddie said. "I'm not marrying anybody right now. All I wanna do is have everybody calm down so I can draw this monster."

A few minutes later, Freddie looked up. "Done," he said, rubbing a cramp out of his hand. The octovark-ephant was complete. It looked pretty disgusting with all eight trunk-like tentacles undulating out from its globular body, but it also looked as though it could take on the swarm of entomons. And maybe even win.

"Nice!" Trevor said, admiring Freddie's work.

"That's awesome." Quincy, Jordan, and Nina triple jinxed each other.

"Could be your best work, buddy." Manny patted his big best friend on the shoulder.

All they had to do was print it and let it soak in water to make sure it grew to its full size. The bigger the bet-ter. They could give it silica to shrink it down later.

While Quincy opened the 3D-printing computer program, Jordan checked the back of the printer and Manny made sure all the settings were correct. Nina plucked a cartridge of 3D-printing goo out of the box.

It was the very last one.

"There's only enough goo for one more monster,"

Nina said. "We have to get this right on the first try."

Freddie placed the drawing of the octovarkephant facedown on the scanner and hit the start button.

Trevor's eyes bugged out as the 3D printer hummed to life.

Goo drizzled from the nozzle and began to give form to the bug-eating monster. It built up from the bottom, layer by layer, detail by detail exactly the way Freddie had drawn it.

Freddie thought about the past two weeks. About his new friends. About how last week's monsters were now their pets. About how one little bug monster had become hundreds, then thousands of monsters. And how they had all come from this weird machine and the 3D-printing goo.

It was completely unreal. And yet it was happening right in front of them.

The machine beeped, and the new monster stood before them on the small platform of the 3D printer.

"He's even grosser and cooler than I imagined." Freddie smiled. "What are we going to name him?"

"I think we should call him Filburt," said Nina.

"That's a terrible name!" Trevor exclaimed.

"I don't know," Manny said, giving it a closer look. "I kinda like Filburt."

"Better come up with something quick, Trevor . . . ," said Freddie. "We gotta grow this bad boy to size."

"Slurp!" Trevor blurted.

"Slurp?" Nina asked.

"Slurp." Freddie nodded. "Slurp's a good name."

"All in favor of Slurp?" Jordan said and raised his hand, as did Freddie, Trevor, and Quincy. "Looks like that's four to two."

Nina went over to Slurp and crouched before him.

"You'll always be Filburt to me."

The monsters then turned their attention toward the new monster. Oddo, Mungo, Kraydon, Yapzilla, and Mega-Q leaned over and inspected the tiny Slurp. They stared at him intently, sniffing him like giant dogs getting to know one another's scents. After a moment, they all nodded in approval. Oddo gave Freddie the thumbs-up with all three hands.

"Welcome to the team, Slurp," said Freddie and gave the monster a pat on his half-aardvark, half-octopus head.

Quincy scooped up the freshly printed critter and cra-dled him in his arm. "Come on, little Slurp, let's turn you into big Slurp!" he said, leading the way upstairs from the basement.

They ran up the stairs with their monsters trailing them. They crowded into the master bathroom with a big shower stall.

Quincy set Slurp down on the tiled floor and stuffed a hand towel over the drain. The octovarkephant just sat there, looking up at them dumbly. Freddie imagined a thought bubble above the monster's head: *Wuz happening, guys?*

Behind them, the door opened and Quincy's grandmother poked her head in the bathroom. Quincy spun around. "Grams? You're home?"

The monsters crammed together in the corner behind the door, trying as best they could to remain out of sight.

"I just got back," said Grams. "Quincy? What's going on here?"

Freddie's heartbeat quickened.

"Hey, Grams," Quincy said. "It's nothing. These are my friends. We're working on a science project. For school."

"Oh," she said, nodding at them as Nina gave her an awkward smile and a wave.

"We'll be done soon, Grams. You don't have to worry about us," Quincy told her.

"Okay, as long as it's for school," she said and stopped in the doorway for a second. "I hope you all get an A." Then she walked out.

Freddie let out a long sigh of relief.

"Your grandma's awesome!" Jordan said.

"Forget about her. Let's get this party started." Quincy twisted both hot and cold knobs on high, but only a tiny trickle of water leaked from the showerhead.

"What's going on?" Freddie asked. "Why is there no water?"

Quincy reached up and unscrewed the showerhead. A few droplets of excess water dribbled down his wrist.

Suddenly, an entomon as big as a king-size candy bar wriggled out of the pipe.

"Ahhh!" Quincy flinched back and the rest of them took a step away from the shower. The first entomon hit the shower floor, followed by three more, falling in rapid succession. Five, ten, twenty more squeezed out like toothpaste.

"Oh, ma jeez!" Freddie squealed as the entomons continued to fall. "They're in the pipes!"

The bug monsters hit the ceramic bath tiles with a clickety-clack, landing all around Slurp.

"Slurp!" Freddie yelled. "Look out!"

The entomons surrounded the brand-new monster and started closing in. Slurp had no way to defend himself, and the entomons were way too big for little Slurp to slurp.

In a blur of fur, Mungo swooped in and pulled Slurp out of the way as another waterfall of bugs fell out of the pipe.

"That's disgusting," Jordan said, a shiver of revulsion rippling through his entire body. "I'm never showering again."

"Now that would be disgusting," said Nina.

"It's like they know we're here," said Quincy. "Like they're targeting us."

"Some species can home in on their prey from vast distances," Trevor informed them. "It's not uncommon in the insect world."

"That's really fascinating and all," Freddie said, "but we need to get to water, you guys!"

Everyone retreated through the bathroom doorway as the thick crunchy insects continued to drop. Freddie slammed the door behind them.

The kids sprinted downstairs to the kitchen, where

Freddie tossed Slurp in the sink. He hit the faucet and a hiss of water spritzed from the nozzle. The water stopped as quickly as it had started. The base of the faucet started to rumble.

"Whoa, what is that?" Quincy said.

The faucet rattled louder and louder until the whole thing popped off with a sharp clank. More bugs popped out.

"AHHH!" shrieked Manny. The entomons were invading from the inside out. "We have to get out of here!" Manny yelled.

Freddie ran to the kitchen window and looked out. The first rays of daylight peeked over the horizon. "I don't think we're going anywhere."

An entomon the size of a baby elephant walked down the middle of the street. *That's the biggest one yet*, Freddie thought, as it crawled easily over a parked car and crumpled the hood.

Across the street, another giant entomon crawled out of a manhole. Another scurried out of a drainpipe. Inside, entomons poured out of Quincy's kitchen sink, skittering up the walls.

"We're trapped!" Trevor exclaimed.

Freddie racked his brain for a plan. How were they supposed to grow Slurp if they couldn't get to any water? He gazed out at the chaos of the insectomonster infestation. Then he noticed it. The words *Go 'Dillos!* up in the sky.

Freddie pointed to the water tower in the distance. "We have to get up there. It's our only shot at making Slurp big."

"But, Freddie, how are we supposed to do that?" Manny asked, looking outside at Quincy's backyard. It was covered in entomons. Not just covered. Swamped. There were thousands upon thousands of them scurrying over everything.

"No way we're going through that," Nina said. "I'm putting my foot down." She lifted her foot and stamped it on the ground.

Splat! The juicy green innards of an entomon squirted from beneath her shoe.

Freddie was getting an idea. "Quincy, do you have speakers and a microphone or something? Anything that can amplify sound."

Quincy's eyes lit up. "My parents have a karaoke machine in the basement!"

Quincy ran downstairs and ran back up carrying the microphone and speaker from his parents' karaoke machine. Freddie tested it and turned up the volume.

"Let me grab one more thing." Quincy ran through the hall to the garage, which was connected to the house. When he came back to the kitchen, he was pulling a red wagon.

"Wait," Manny said. "So what's the plan?"

"We're gonna put the *reech* back in Yapzilla's screech," Freddie said.

The kids all gave him a puzzled look.

"We're going to amplify Yapzilla's screech and use it as a kind of shield so we can make it to the water tower."

"You're sure that's going to work?" Manny asked skeptically.

"She did it back at the cornfield," Freddie told them. "It was like a sonic forcefield."

"All right then," Nina said, looking at Yapzilla. "Let's do this, girl."

They all got ready. Jordan straightened the gemstone magnifier on Kraydon's forehead. While Freddie and Quincy arranged the speakers in the wagon, Oddo and Mungo opened the drawer next to the sink and armed themselves with forks and knives.

While Freddie finished hooking up the microphone to the speakers, Quincy ran out of the room and came back with a bag of cotton balls. "For our ears," he said, and passed them out.

"Wait, how are we going to turn on the speakers unless we have a power source?" Trevor asked.

"We do have a power source!" Quincy said, nodding at Mega-Q.

Mega-Q slithered next to the red wagon and charged

the speakers with his electric blue current.

Nina grabbed a shovel and two cans of bug repellent from Quincy's garage, and Manny chose a metal trash can lid for a shield and a pickax off the wall. Freddie stuck with the lacrosse stick he still had from Trevor's house. Jordan found a Weedwacker in the corner, and Quincy opted for two tennis rackets. Trevor picked up a rake with a metal head. They were ready to roll.

Freddie called Yapzilla to come over: "You're up, Yap!" He gave her the microphone. "When we go outside," he instructed her, "I want you to shriek as loud as you can nonstop, okay?"

Yapzilla took the microphone in her talons and nodded. The twin-necked monster preened. Even in the middle of a bug attack, she loved to be the center of attention.

The kids put the cotton into their ears and gave Yapzilla the signal.

Without wasting another second, they threw the back door open and rolled the wagon outside into the bug-filled bedlam.

Yapzilla the double-necked monster screeched into

the microphone. The high-pitched shriek was amplified through the speakers. Just as Freddie had predicted, the ear-piercing noise formed a sonic force field. The entomons skittered back, giving the kids a buffer to move through the swarm untouched.

"You're doing great, Yap!" Freddie called to her as they fled through Quincy's backyard and down his driveway.

Yapzilla held her shrieking opera note, keeping up the sonic force field.

In the dim light of the sunrise, they made their way across the street. They moved through the thick of the entoswarm until they reached the flat dirt field where the water tower looked over their town.

At the fringe of Yapzilla's sonic barrier, the monster bugs' jaws snapped and snarled. Above the swarm, the original parentomons flew over their army of bug monsters. How long had it been since they'd sprouted wings? How much longer until the entire swarm grew wings, too?

The kids weren't waiting around to find out. They were going to stop this infestation once and for all.

When they reached the water tower, Freddie slipped Slurp into his pocket and began climbing the metal ladder. "Don't look down, don't look down," he said to himself. But when he reached the top, he looked down at his friends. They seemed so tiny.

Yapzilla's screech continued to keep the thick mass of bugs from attacking them. She belted out a high-pitched F sharp into the karaoke microphone.

While Mega-Q zapped the bugs, Kraydon turned his one-eyed gaze at the oncoming onslaught. Around the perimeter of Yapzilla's sonic shriek barrier, the wall of stone-frozen entomons rose up. The more bugs Kraydon hit, the taller the stone wall became. The bigger bugs hardened in the wall, looking like gargoyles from another planet.

Let's hope they can keep it up until I get down, Freddie thought.

Freddie reached the top and pulled Slurp out of his pocket. With both hands, he tried to crank open the hatch on the side of the water tank. It wouldn't budge.

"It won't open!" he called down.

Quickly, Oddo and Mungo scaled the water tower's ladder and met Freddie at the top. The two of them grabbed the metal valve wheel and tried to turn it. Freddie gave one final twist, and the hatch popped open.

"You'll be okay, little buddy!" Freddie tossed Slurp

into the open water tower. The little octovarkephant monster made a splash, and Freddie shut the small door.

He began to climb down with Oddo and Mungo above him. But Freddie soon realized that climbing down was much scarier than climbing up. He forced himself to go slow, but he could tell from the rumble inside the water tower that their monster was growing fast.

Just then, Freddie felt the ladder jerk. He clung to the ladder as their monster started to outgrow the water tank. The metal banged and dented outward. A loud creak tore through the air, and the whole tower shifted.

Freddie's body stiffened with fear.

"Holy—"

CRRRRR-ACK!

The top of the tower exploded, and Slurp's tentacular snouts burst out. A huge gash zigzagged through the giant metal tank. Water spewed out from the crack and rained down in a flailing puddle.

"Look out below!" Freddie shouted to his friends. They jumped out of the way as Slurp burst free and hit the entomon-covered ground with a wet *thwock*.

A wave of water fell from the sky and spattered onto the front lines of the entomon horde. They started to grow.

"Oh no!" Quincy shouted as entomons soaked up the water. In a flash of electricity Mega-Q zapped the waterlogged swarm. The electrocuted entomons dropped into a scorched, motionless heap.

But they weren't the only thing that was dead: the speakers had shorted out, too. Yapzilla's screech was drowned out by the sound of the bugs' creepy chittering.

The bugs were closing in.

"C'mon, Slurp! Go get 'em!" Freddie shouted from the ladder.

The massive octovarkephant stood up to his full height. Slurp let out a voracious elephantine roar that sounded like a humongous trumpet. He was ready for battle.

Their monster's huge waggling snouts were like vacuum cleaners, and he began to suck up the entomons with incredible speed.

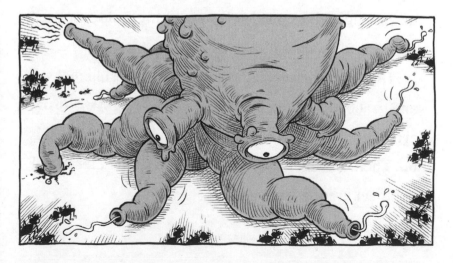

We might actually win this thing, Freddie dared to hope as he kept climbing down one rung at a time.

Just then, the ladder began to shake. Freddie looked down. The entomons were climbing up the unsteady structure, scrabbling straight for him.

Mungo scampered down, positioning himself on the ladder, getting ready to defend Freddie from the attacking bugs.

On the ground below, Slurp's massive tentacles swung across the dirt field, batting away the bigger entomons, sucking up the smaller hordes. One of his eight appendages slammed into the base of the tower and sent a vibration ringing up to the top.

The water tower lurched like it was going to topple. Freddie whipped to the left, his fingers slipping. He lost his footing and dropped to the next rung, holding on for dear life with one arm.

Higher up on the same ladder, Oddo reached down and grabbed Freddie by the wrist with one of his furry arms. Freddie hung from the monster's grasp, looking up. Their eyes met. Oddo looked scared but determined not to let Freddie go.

The tower creaked loudly and shifted again.

"Ruh-roh," Oddo rumbled.

Everything felt like slow motion as the tower groaned and tipped like a tree going timber. Freddie's face froze in shock as he dropped into a free fall. He twisted in the air, soaring toward the ground headfirst. He could see Oddo and Mungo skydiving just in front of him. A smattering of entomons speckled the air around them.

Slurp was directly below them.

Mungo reached out and ate a bug in midair.

"Yum yums," he chirruped, his ears waving in the wind.

The octovarkephant swiveled his eyes up at the falling threesome: Freddie, Oddo, and Mungo. Slurp extended one of his tentacles toward the sky, and Freddie could see right into the suck hole of its slurping snout.

Please, don't slurp me, Slurp, Freddie thought, *Slurp, don't slurp me, please!*

SPLUNK!

Freddie felt the cushion of the octovarkephant's smushy trunktacle, breaking his fall. He bounced off the gigantic monster's tough skin and belly flopped onto the ground. Oddo and Mungo landed on Slurp's back and slid down to the ground.

Freddie's knees hurt, but at least he was in one piece. He hobbled in place for a second and shook off the pain.

Manny and Jordan raced over to protect Freddie from the swarm.

Freddie picked up his lacrosse stick and scooped a slew of entomons over his shoulder. Manny, armed with a trash can lid and a pickax, fought off a warthog-size bug. He blocked its snapping jaws with his makeshift shield. The beastly insect's mandibles clashed against the metal, and Manny slammed the pickax down on the monster bug's noggin. The ravenous insect's head caved in and neon-green sludge spurted out. The ferocious creature's legs collapsed and it went still.

"Jordan, look out!" Nina shouted and pointed at Jordan's foot.

One of the entomons clamped its pincers into the skin of Jordan's leg. "Yow!" Jordan yipped as a trickle of blood slid down his calf muscle. Jordan swept the bug monster off his leg and stomped it into the ground.

Slurp trumpeted another roaring elephant shriek and went back to slurping up oodles of entomonsters.

But some of the bugs were just too big.

Oddo and Mungo were like two master ninjas taking on a whole mob of street thugs. Mungo body-slammed five entomons in the blink of an eye, and Oddo donkey kicked two entomons in the face while punching another one in the snout with his extra arm.

On the other side of Slurp, Quincy was fighting, thwapping the bugs to and fro with dual tennis rackets.

Mega-Q zipped around his feet. He was like the world's best bug zapper, electrocuting entomons left and right.

Trevor jabbed his rake in the face of a massive, snarling entomonster.

Next to Quincy, Nina stabbed her shovel into a gargantuan entobug, let go of the handle, spun on her heels, and sprayed an incoming flock of little skittering entomons with two cans of Off! that she pulled out of her waistband at the same time. Yapzilla squawked and unleashed two bursts of fire at the chemical spray. Her tongue flickered and she spat a spiral stream of flames. The aerosol spray lit like a torch and scorched the front lines, grilling the entomons to a crisp. The dead bugs blazed in a lime-green flame as their juicy guts burned like gasoline.

Kraydon shot his spiral gaze through the amplifier. A chunk of bugs solidified, and he clobbered them with his club tail.

Oddo dropped back into some kind of break-dance move and sent two entomons flying. Mega-Q zapped four more in rapid suc-cession, and Kraydon froze a newly replicated batch before blasting the bug statues to smith-ereens.

All the while, Slurp's colossal tentacles swept across the ground, sucking up the entomons like the nozzles of a massive vacuum cleaner.

"Come on, you entofreaks! Come and get some!" Jordan pulled the ripcord on the Weedwacker and its plastic blades whizzed.

Jordan shredded the monster bugs, spraying lime-green guts into the air like a sprinkler on full blast.

Fighting alongside Oddo and Mungo, Freddie swatted an oncoming entomon with the lacrosse stick, flipping the large bug monster on its back. He raised the butt end of the stick over his head and brought it down with a crunchy splat, impaling the colossal insect with the shaft.

But the bugs just kept on coming.

Freddie took in the unwinnable battle before him.

For as far as he could see, there was nothing green. Not a tree, not a shrub, nor a single blade of grass. Freddie figured that was a bad thing for several obvious reasons.

"Hey, Trevor, what did you say happens when all these things eat all the plant life?" Freddie asked, shouting through the bug monster mayhem.

"Then they'll move on to us . . . ," Trevor shouted back.

"Great," Freddie replied. "Just great."

Out of the corner of his eye he saw the parentomon duo buzzing over the swarm.

The flying parentomons hovered in the air above the other bugs. It seemed as though they were orchestrating the swarm's movements somehow, conducting a symphony of chaos.

"They're controlling them," Freddie called out to his friends.

"They must be operating under one singular hive mind . . . ," Trevor said in awe of the insects.

"I think I'm *getting* hives. . . ." Nina groaned as she bashed in the head of the umpteenth entomon.

And that's when it happened.

The entomons began to gather, crawling on top of one another. They crawled up and up and up. Soon, they looked like a giant bug Godzilla, with arms and legs and a head. Their beetle shells looked like shiny black scales. All together, the bugs were nearly as tall as the water tower. They were certainly bigger than Slurp.

The bugs had turned into one enormous monster.

Slurp didn't have a chance against something like that.

"If we can take out the ringleaders, then maybe we can stop that thing," Freddie yelled. "That's our only chance!"

The flying parentomons circled the gigantic bug monster, buzzing around Freddie's eyes, making it difficult to see what Trevor was doing. Slurp raised two of his tentacles, but it seemed useless.

I should have given him more eyes, Freddie thought.

"He needs help!" Manny shouted to their monsters.

Kraydon, Yapzilla, and Mega-Q tried to defend Slurp. They shot off zaps and shrieks and flames.

The parentomons hovered over the writhing Godzilla-shaped swarm.

"I have to go to them," Trevor said. "I'm not afraid."

"They'll kill you!" Jordan said.

"They won't hurt me," Trevor said. "They know me. I love them."

Freddie nodded at Trevor. He understood that Trevor needed to do this—for them, for their town, but also for himself. To prove that he was taking responsibility for what had gone wrong. Freddie had stood in those shoes before.

"If you're gonna go, then go!" Nina yelled, stomping out another flock of entomons.

They watched as Trevor waded toward the giant entomon monster. The monster reached down its hand and scooped up Trevor. The entomons began to cover his entire body, but Trevor didn't look afraid.

"Are we sure this is a good idea?" Manny asked.

"Hello, my darlings!" Trevor yelled up to the parentomons and raised his arms.

Freddie could barely make out Trevor through the swarm. He was just standing there, arms raised. Freddie couldn't quite tell, but it looked like there were tears streaming down Trevor's face. He watched as the flying parent bugs descended and landed on Trevor's arms. The winged parentomons fluttered like crazy on his

wrists. Then the swarm thickened and Trevor disappeared from view.

"What's he doing?!" Nina shouted.

"He's not stopping them!" yelled Jordan. "He's just letting them flap around!"

A cloud covered sun and a dark thought crossed Freddie's mind. Had this been Trevor's plan the whole time? The good guys lose, and the bugs take over the world with Trevor as their king?

"Trevor!" Freddie, Manny, and Quincy all screamed at the top of their lungs in a three-way jinx.

Come on, Trevor, thought Freddie, wanting to believe in the good, but all he could do was watch in horror as the legion of bugs loomed over them in the shape of a Kaiju.

"Trevor, do it already!" Nina shrieked almost louder than Yapzilla.

"Do it, you little twerp!" Jordan yelled through the wall of entomons rising before them.

"Freddie, if we don't get out of this," Manny said, talking faster than a third grader on a sugar high. "You're my best friend! I love you, man!"

"I love you, too, buddy!" Freddie yelled back over the chattering buzz of the swarm. "You're my best friend, too."

The bug swarm reared up like a Godzilla-shaped tsunami, covering the kids in a pitch-black shadow,

blocking the faint light of daybreak.

The gigantic mass of monster bugs looked ready to slam down over the kids.

"Look out!" Jordan cried.

"Run!" Quincy shouted. But there was nowhere to run.

Freddie froze in place and covered his head with his arms.

Suddenly all the entomons dropped out of their

monstrous formation and hit the ground like a hail-storm. The bugs were loopy and directionless. They wandered around on the ground.

Slurp quickly slurped up the rest of the entomons.

"Get 'em!" Freddie said, and they all charged forward. The kids and their monsters destroyed the few remaining entomons that were too big for Slurp to slurp.

When the octovarkephant's eight ent-eater trunks finished vacuuming the swarm, there wasn't a single bug left.

"Is everyone okay?" Manny asked.

"We did it!" Jordan screamed.

"Wait a second," Nina said. "Where's Trevor?"

Freddie turned around and saw Trevor down on his knees, about ten yards away.

The two original parentomons lay at his feet, crushed by Trevor's shoe. In the dawn light, a twinkle appeared on Trevor's cheek as a tear ran down the side of his face. His twin bugs were now nothing more than two green splotches in the dirt.

"What's the matter with you, Trevor?!" Quincy

shouted at him. "Why did you wait so long?"

"What do you want from me?" Trevor shouted back. "I did the right thing! I killed them, didn't I? I killed my precious—" He choked on his next words.

"You could have gotten us all killed, hesitating like that!" Jordan shouted. "What's more important? Your friends, or a couple of stupid bugs?"

"Is that what you think?" Trevor asked, his eyes brimming with tears.

Freddie turned to the rest of the gang. "Guys, go easy on him—we won . . . and he helped us. . . ."

"If by helping us you mean scared me half to death, then, yeah," said Nina. "You were a real gem, Trevor!"

Freddie jogged over to Trevor and helped him to his feet. "It's okay, buddy," he said. "You did the right thing."

"I know." Trevor sniffled. "I know. . . ."

"I know it wasn't easy . . . ," Freddie started to say, when his whole body tensed up.

They felt a rumble. The earth began to tremble.

"What was that?" Manny said.

Then it broke through the damp soil where the water

from the tower had soaked into the ground. First the mandibular snout formed, next the squiggly forearms bristled with antennae, then the shiny blue-black shell. Its pincers were longer than Freddie was tall.

One of Slurp's tentacles shot out over the kids' heads and latched on to the side of the monster bug. The octo-varkephant snorted hard, but the thing was too massive to suck up.

Then, the gargantuan entomon started to split into two.

"What . . . is . . . happening . . . ," Nina said in shock.

"It's replicating again!" Quincy said.

The behemoth bug split in half to display a newly hatched enormo-insect. It was . . . huge.

Mungo saw the thing and barfed. It was too gross for even Mungo to handle.

"He's going for Slurp!" Freddie yelped as the monster lunged forward.

Slurp raised its waggling limb to block the oncoming beast.

The entomon's mandibles clicked shut and snipped Slurp's tentacle in half.

Slurp wailed as the tip of his tentacle dropped in the dirt. It kept wiggling, like it was still alive. The entomon went up on its hind legs and roared. The thing was as big as a triceratops.

Suddenly Trevor jumped to his feet. "I'll prove to you guys whose side I'm on, once and for all!" Trevor raced over and pounced onto the back of the entomon.

"Trevor, don't!" Freddie shouted, but Trevor was already on the bug like a bull rider. Freddie turned to his friends. "You see what happens when you mess with people?"

They all hung their heads a little.

Manny looked up, then sprang into action. "Hold on, Trevor. We're going to save you!" They all took off, sprinting to help their new friend, who was hanging on for dear life, jostling back and forth on the back of the gigantic entomon.

As they ran over to help Trevor, their monsters converged on the first massive bug monster. Yapzilla spewed fire at the humongous beastie, and Mega-Q zapped it with bolt after bolt of blue electricity.

Kraydon swung his spiked tail and knocked out the big bug's front two legs. The entomon nose-dived into the ground. When the bug went down, Oddo jumped into the air and rolled into a ball. The big fuzzball came down hard on the big bug, making a dent in the side of its hard outer shell.

The entomonster squealed as Oddo bounced off, and Mungo swooped in as the enormous bug collapsed to one side.

The huge bug slumped down and went still.

"One down!" Jordan shouted with glee as they surrounded the second entomon.

Trevor was still in trouble with the other monster bug. "Whoa!" he shouted from the back of the bucking insect.

The entomonster scuttled backward and Trevor flew forward over its head. Trevor's pants leg got caught in the monster's antennae. He hung upside down, waving his arms for help.

Freddie sprinted toward the bug monster and jumped. He reached up and grabbed the monster's pincer.

SNAP!

Freddie fell to the ground, still holding the pincer, which was no longer attached to the monster. Trevor fell next to him, and a waterfall of green slime guts poured down on them.

The final entomon reared back, and its pointy feet lifted over Freddie and Trevor.

"Freddie, Trevor, watch out!" Nina screamed.

Just then, one of Slurp's tentacles swept across the ground and knocked out the monster bug's back legs. It flipped over onto its back, its giant, spindly legs waving in the air.

Jordan, Nina, and Quincy ran over. They pummeled the bug monster's soft underbelly with their sticks and rackets until the bug went limp.

"Woo-hoo!" Jordan whooped, and high-fived Freddie, Manny, and Quincy, then spun around and did an end zone dance.

But there wasn't much time for celebration.

"You guys, get over here, quick!" Nina called out. She stood next to Slurp, examining the monster. He was slumped over and looked sick. The giant eight-snouted creature was wheezing through his trunks. "Something's wrong with Filburt!"

"You mean Slurp."

"No, I mean Filburt," she said tersely.

The octovarkephant trumpeted a giant belch and then dropped into a heap.

Slurp did not look good.

He slunk on the ground. The gurgle of his stomach was audible up to a good ten feet away. The creature emitted a foul, ghastly stench.

Manny, Jordan, and Quincy all rushed over to Slurp and gathered before him.

"You think he ate too much?" asked Jordan.

"No, I think he ate the perfect amount," Quincy said. "There's not a single entomon left."

"Maybe he just needs time to digest . . . ," Manny said.

Freddie limped over to Trevor, trying not to slip on the bug guts.

"Maybe if we shrink him down it'll be okay?" Manny suggested.

"Maybe . . ." Quincy pulled out the tin of silica slugs and dumped the rest of the silica into the giant octovarkephant monster's mouth.

They waited for the silica to kick in. Slurp's body vibrated and jiggled as it shrank to a pint-sized version of his gigantic self.

Come on, Slurp, Freddie thought. *Don't quit on us now.*

They waited for the monster to come back to life . . . but it was no use.

Slurp sagged, then melted into a pink puddle and faded into the dirt.

He was gone.

"Filburt!" Nina cried, her eyes welling up with tears.

"His name's not Filburt, it's Slurp," Trevor said, tears streaming down his face.

"We'll never forget what you did here today,

Slurp . . . ," Freddie said sadly.

"The world owes you a debt of gratitude it will never even know it has to repay," Quincy said solemnly as he stood over the pink puddle.

"You were the man, Slurp . . . ," Jordan said, a single tear falling down his cheek.

"Yeah, you were the man-ster," Manny said. "Get it? Like mon-ster?"

"Okay, how about a compromise," Nina said. "How about we make him a gravestone and we'll write 'Filburt von Slurpenstein, the one and only.'"

"He was a monster of destiny," Quincy said. "Destined for greatness. A short life, but an important one . . ."

Trevor's face drooped into a sad pout.

"Are you okay, Trevor?" Freddie said. "We still won. Slurp served his purpose."

"No, I'm not okay," Trevor said. "And now I don't have any bugs or any friends."

"Well, I can't do anything about the bugs . . . but we'll be your friends," Freddie said to him.

"That depends . . . How are you at doing other

people's homework for them?" Jordan asked.

"How are you at doing chores?" Nina asked.

"What about foot massages?" Manny said.

"We're just messing with you, Trevor," said Jordan. "Friends wouldn't make you do all that stuff."

"I don't really know that much about having friends, I guess," Trevor said.

"Don't worry," said Quincy. "We'll teach you."

"I'm not sure Quincy will be the best teacher," said Nina. "So you may want to listen to me and Jordan on that one."

Trevor let out a chuckle. "Okay."

"Freddie and Manny aren't bad friends to have either," Jordan said.

"They're pretty cool," Quincy said to Trevor. "All I'm saying is stick with me and you'll learn everything you need to know."

"Looks like you just became a member of monster club!" Freddie gave the small kid a pat on the shoulder.

"Thanks, guys," Trevor said. "Thank you for giving me a chance."

The sound of police and ambulance sirens whooped faintly in the distance. Freddie listened closely and heard the muffled chop of a helicopter. The sun was poking halfway over the mountain range in the distance, and his town was waking up to another round of monster destruction.

"I think we better get outta here," he said. "Quick."

They all hopped on the backs of their monsters and galloped home toward the rising sun.

They took the long way home, down a winding back road, to avoid being seen by any neighbors. The monster night was over and the entomons had been exterminated.

As they passed by the park, they caught a glimpse of a man and a woman in spandex outfits and running shoes. But they weren't jogging. They were looking at the bare pine trees and the bug-ravaged grass, scratching their heads.

A few blocks later, a woman in her bathrobe stood outside, looking at her dirt yard. She rubbed her chin, puzzling how all her grass could have disappeared overnight.

She was so confused about her lawn she didn't even notice the caravan of monsters turning the corner one block over.

Freddie could only imagine what the neighbors were thinking. Unless they knew about a 3D printer capable of making monsters, he was pretty sure their secret would be safe.

And who would believe that anyway?

When the kids arrived back at Quincy's house, they tiptoed through the back door. Quincy followed with a towel to wipe up all the monsters' dirty paw prints. Thankfully all the entomonsters had left the house in one piece. Except for a few entomons that they'd stomped, there weren't any bugs left in sight.

There was one last thing they had to do.

"We need to shrink these guys back down," Quincy said, gesturing to their five super-size monsters crowding in the kitchen.

"Will it work?" Freddie asked.

"If they can grow again, why can't they shrink again?" Quincy replied. "There's only one way to find out."

"Cool, feed them the slugs," Manny said.

"Um . . . well, I used the last of the silica on Slurp. I don't know if we have any more," Quincy said.

"Where is your mom's closet?" Nina asked.

"Upstairs, last door on the left . . . ," Quincy said, a confused look on his face. "Just don't bother my grandma, okay?"

Nina bounded out of the kitchen and raced up the staircase. When she came back, she was holding a shoe

box with five or six silica packets inside. "This oughta do it," she said. "Those packets usually come in shoe boxes, too."

The kids took the packets and cut them open, then pressed the pellets into a few gummi worms.

Freddie handed out the silica-spackled candy, and the monsters looked at him like they wanted to have nothing to do with it.

"I know it's not fun to shrink, but if you guys don't take this, then people will try to take you away from us," he said. "Do you understand?"

The monsters nodded and ate the silica treats a little sadly.

Kraydon started to shake, followed by Oddo and Mungo, Yapzilla and Mega-Q, all of them convulsing

rapidly. The floor vibrated as the large monsters shrank back down to their pet-size mini-selves.

"I guess we'll just have to give them the silica every two weeks or so," Quincy said.

"Yum yums," Mungo said, because that's what Mungo always said.

"We need to destroy that printer, too," Freddie said.

"Why would we do that?" Quincy asked. "We don't even understand how it works yet."

"So what?" Freddie said. "We know what it does. The destruction that it's capable of."

"I agree," Nina said as she brushed the bug legs and gunk out of Oddo's fur. "It's too powerful to keep around. Nothing but trouble."

"You know," Manny said, "maybe it's not the printer or the goo that has the power. It's you, Freddie. Your drawings have life in them way before they ever go through some printer."

There were good things and bad things that happened because of that 3D printer. People had been scared and some stuff had been destroyed. And, after all, they wouldn't have their supercool monster amigos if it weren't for the printer. And there was no way they'd all be friends right now.

"Thanks, Manny," Freddie said, "but I don't care about any of that. We have to make sure it never happens again, and the only way to do that is to destroy it."

Freddie went to the basement, followed by Manny, Nina, Jordan, Trevor, and their shrunken minimonsters.

They gathered around the worktable with the 3D printer on it.

Quincy took a stand in front of the printer with Mega-Q beside him. "Anyone who tries to touch this printer is going to have to go through me and Mega. . . ."

"I don't think Kraydon cares," Manny said.

"Huh?" Quincy turned around.

Kraydon's eye started to swirl and quickly turned the whole printer to solid rock.

"Hey, what are you doing?" Quincy said. "Turn it back, right now."

Kraydon crossed his arms and shook his head.

"I'm serious. Turn it back, or else . . ."

"Or else what?" Jordan asked. "Don't talk to my monster like that."

"Yeah, Quincy," Nina said. "Quit acting so bossy."

"Fine, it can be made of stone, so no one can use it, but let's not destroy it. Not yet."

Kraydon nodded at Jordan. The minimonster pointed to his eyeball then shook his finger no at the 3D printer.

"I'm pretty sure he understands," Jordan said.

Quincy placed the frozen-solid 3D printer on a shelf behind a bunch of board games and old science experiments. They all went back up to the first floor.

Freddie and Manny stood side by side at the sink and washed all the bug guts off their arms and legs. Manny didn't look like someone who had just saved their town

161

from total insect Armageddon. He looked more like a kid whose dog just died on Christmas.

"You okay, man?" Freddie asked.

Manny looked. "I'm all right," he said. "Just a little tired. Long night."

"Yeah," Freddie replied quietly. "Long night."

But that isn't it, Freddie thought, and then it dawned on him. Actually, the realization punched him right in the gut.

Today is Manny's birthday!

Right until this second, Freddie had completely forgotten. He felt terrible. Freddie had intended to plan Manny's birthday celebration weeks in advance. It must have been bothering Manny for days that Freddie hadn't told him the plan yet. There had been so much going on: new school, new friends, new monsters. It had simply slipped his mind.

Freddie finished washing up and left Manny at the sink. He quietly called Jordan, Nina, Quincy, and Trevor into the pantry off the kitchen. He took a deep breath and told them the deal.

"You forgot his b—?" Nina started to say way too loud, and Freddie clamped his hand over her mouth.

"Shhhhh!" Freddie said. "He doesn't know I forgot yet."

"We have to do something," Trevor said.

"I have a couple boxes of cupcakes," Quincy said. "They're store-bought, but, my oh my, are they delicious."

"What about decorations?" Nina asked.

"I think my mom keeps some streamers and party hats somewhere around here. I can ask her," Quincy said. "Maybe some balloons, too."

"What about candles?" Nina asked.

"Yep." Quincy nodded. "We got candles."

"Okay, awesome," Freddie said. "Quincy, you and Jordan will get the food. Nina and I will take care of the decorations."

"What do I do?" Trevor asked.

"You go keep Manny occupied," Freddie said. "Make sure he doesn't come in the living room."

With that, Nina and Freddie went into the living

room and hung the streamers. They showed Oddo and Kraydon how to blow up the balloons, and Mega-Q used some static electricity to make them cling all over the ceiling and the walls.

Jordan and Quincy came in holding a platter of cupcakes, one of them with a candle sticking out of the middle. "I can't find any matches," Quincy said.

Yapzilla scampered over and lit the candle with her torch breath.

"Okay, Trevor," Freddie said. "We're ready!"

A few seconds later, Trevor and Manny walked through the streamers hanging down in the doorway.

Mungo handed Manny a cupcake. "Yum yums," he said.

Manny's smile stretched ear to ear. "I thought you guys forgot," he said, as they sang an out-of-tune rendition of the happy birthday song.

"Okay, okay, stop it!" Manny said. "You guys are terrible singers."

"Except for me," Nina said.

"Except for Nina," Manny acknowledged, blowing out

the candle. "Thanks, guys . . . this means a lot." He looked
at Freddie for a long moment. "Freddie, you're my best
friend in the whole wide world, but all of you are the best
friends a guy could ask to go into battle with." Then he
stared down at their minimonsters. "And you dudes, too."

For the first time since the entomons attacked, Freddie smiled.

"Let's eat," Manny said. "I'm starving!"

Freddie sank his teeth into the frosted cake and felt
a loud crunch.

"Ugh! Gross!" Freddie said. An entomon leg stuck out of the cake.

"Hey, at least it's dead, right?" Manny said. He handed Freddie a piece of his own cupcake.

"Aw, thanks, dude," Freddie said to his best friend. It was the tastiest cupcake Freddie had ever eaten.

A few seconds later, he could hear the creak of footsteps coming down the staircase. The kids and monsters paused and turned toward the living room doorway. Quincy's grandmother stood in her nightie and a pair of slippers, staring at them.

"Are you and your friends done with your science project, Quincy?" she asked, breaking the silence.

"Umm . . . yeah, Grandma," Quincy said, waiting to see if she would notice the minimonsters who had all frozen in odd postures around the living room.

Grams did not notice. "Will you get an A?" she asked instead.

"We will," Freddie spoke up with a mouthful of cupcake. "Actually I think we're going to get an A plus."

"Oh, that's wonderful!" she said. "I'm going to go

make myself a cup of tea."

They held their breaths until she was out of the room.

Then the kids—and their monsters—let out a sigh of relief.

Freddie looked at his friends and smiled. They'd saved their town and probably the whole world. It wasn't the first time, but he hoped it would be the last. He couldn't know for sure.

In the meantime, Freddie went back to his cupcake.

Acknowledgments

Enormous thanks to everyone at Alloy and Harper for helping me shrink down this monster book to a tamable size. To my editors, Hayley and Alice, thank you for all your great ideas and helping me find the logic in 3D-printed self-replicating monster bugs; to Emilia, thanks for having faith that each draft will be bigger and better and more monstrous than the last; and to Josh and Sara and Les, thanks as always for brainstorming with me and getting this project on track. And thank you to my agent, Ryan, for all his help and guidance along the monster-ridden way. And most important, Jenny, my love, who's always there, and who makes me a better writer. You are.